ICE BLONDE

ALSO BY ELAINE VIETS

ANGELA RICHMAN,
DEATH INVESTIGATOR
Brain Storm
Fire and Ashes
Ice Blonde (Novella) *

FRANCESCA VIERLING MYSTERIES
Backstab
Rubout
The Pink Flamingo Murders
Doc in the Box

JOSIE MARCUS, MYSTERY SHOPPER
Dying in Style *
High Heels Are Murder *
Accessory to Murder *
Murder with All the Trimmings *
The Fashion Hound Murders *
An Uplifting Murder *
Death on a Platter *
Murder Is a Piece of Cake *
Fixing to Die *
A Dog Gone Murder *

DEAD-END JOB MYSTERIES
Shop till You Drop *
Murder Between the Covers *
Dying to Call You *
Just Murdered *
Murder Unleashed *
Murder with Reservations *
Clubbed to Death *
Killer Cuts *
Half-Price Homicide *
Pumped for Murder *
Final Sail *
Board Stiff *
Catnapped! *
Checked Out
The Art of Murder
Killer Blonde (Novella)

*Available as a JABberwocky eBook edition

ICE BLONDE

AN ANGELA RICHMAN, DEATH INVESTIGATOR NOVELLA

ELAINE VIETS

Published by JABberwocky Literary Agency, Inc.

ICE BLONDE

This paperback edition published in 2018 by JABberwocky Literary Agency, Inc.
www.awfulagent.com/ebooks

Cover design by Tara O'Shea
http://www.fringe-elements.com/

Cover images © Dreamstime

ISBN 978-1-625673-62-6

For medicolegal death investigator Mary Fran Ernst, who set the standards for this profession – and aimed high.

CHAPTER 1

Tuesday, December 27, 6:30 a.m.

Midge LaRouche was the last person I expected to find on my door-step two days after Christmas. Especially at the insane hour of six-thirty. Midge's confident upper-crust bray was muted to a tentative peep. Her husband, Prentice, stood behind her as if he feared she'd run away.

Forty, fit, and tanned, the LaRouches were supposed to be in Tel-luride, Colorado, the week between Christmas and New Year's Day. Everyone who was anyone fled Chouteau County, Missouri, to bake on a beach or swoosh down the slopes during the holidays.

"Is something wrong?" I asked. The LaRouches have never been to my house. The mere mention of my job scared the hell out of them. I'm Angela Richman, a Chouteau County death investigator. I work for the medical examiner, and I'm called to the scene of all the county's homicides and unexplained deaths. That's why Midge's next words were so ominous.

"Our daughter didn't come home last night." Midge's eyes filled with tears. Her nose was red, but I didn't know if that was the extreme cold, or if she'd been crying. "Juliet's only sixteen. She promised she'd be home from the party by midnight." She brushed her blonde bangs out of the way, and dabbed at her eyes with her ski mittens.

"Juliet's very reliable," Prentice said, as if he was recommending the girl for a job. "We've never had a problem. When we give her a time, she's home. The party was at Arabella Du Pres's house – her cousin. Bella's parents were the chaperones. That's why we don't understand what went wrong.

"When Juliet wasn't home by one o'clock, our housekeeper called the Du Pres home and discovered our daughter had left more than an hour ago," he said. "Juliet should have been home in ten minutes – fifteen at the most. Mrs. Ellis called the police and the hospitals, but Juliet hadn't been in an accident. That's when she called us, and we came straight home.

"Thank gawd we didn't have to fly commercial," Prentice drawled. "Our little plane had us home by five this morning."

The blond couple was dressed for the slopes in ski togs and sun goggles, and they needed them. I could see Midge's breath. I shivered and pulled my old brown robe tighter. His daughter's missing on the coldest day of the year and he's bragging that he flew on his private jet.

"We'll freeze to death out here on the porch. Come inside."

Midge burst into tears and I realized my words were tactless. "That's why we're so worried," she said. I was astonished Midge remembered to wipe her feet on the mat. "I'm so afraid it's too late for my little girl. Juliet isn't dressed for this."

Midge and her husband followed me to my warm kitchen, bringing their own sub-zero zone with them like a prisoner in custody.

The LaRouches sat at the table, pulling off their mittens and unzipping their jackets. As I fussed with the coffee maker, my sleep-stunned brain struggled to picture Juliet. The girl was probably blonde and pretty, like most of the local rich kids. She'd have the meticulous good grooming that passed for beauty: straight teeth, steam-cleaned skin, shiny hair. But I couldn't remember what she looked like.

"What was Juliet wearing?" I asked.

"She left the house in a blue velvet strapless dress, high heels and a light-blue velveteen jacket," Midge said. "She had her cell phone in a little silver purse."

"That's all?" The coffee maker erupted in burbles and belches, giving my kitchen the comforting aroma of fresh coffee.

"She refused to wear her boots, heavy coat, or even gloves," Midge said. "She said it would spoil her look."

"I remember being like that at her age." I smiled.

"I do, too," Midge said. "But now her vanity could … could …"
I mentally finished the sentence Midge couldn't say: *could kill her.*
Juliet's mother was fighting hard not to cry again, but tears spilled down her cheeks. Prentice handed her a snowy pocket handkerchief, and she dabbed her eyes. "There, there, old girl." He patted her shoulder. "I'm sure she's staying at a friend's house and this is all a misunderstanding."

"I assume you've called her friends," I said.

"Of course," Prentice said. "No one's seen Juliet since she left the party."

"And the police?"

"They've already launched their own search and they're organizing the volunteer search parties—the scouts, school groups, churches. The search is countywide."

Chouteau County is ten square miles of white privilege about thirty miles west of St. Louis. Our police exist to protect and serve this enchanted enclave. Chouteau Forest is the main town, surrounded by forested estates. Toonerville, the blue-collar section, is where most of the Forest workers live.

I was afraid the search was hopeless. People like the LaRouches were barricaded behind wrought-iron gates in their late nineteenth-century mansions. Their estates were sprinkled with horse barns, guest houses, pool houses, topiary mazes, sheds, and storage buildings. I lived on old Reggie Du Pres's estate, in a former guest house that was my parents' home. It would take a whole day to search that vast complex. Toonerville was a patchwork of modest houses with small backyards, garages and tool sheds – each one a potential hiding place.

Midge said, "We also called the Hobarts, the Du Presses, the DeMuns – no one's seen her, but they're organizing search parties, too."

"I'll get dressed and join them," I said.

"That's not why we're here," Midge said. "We wouldn't expect you to search. Not with your health issues." I saw her avid eyes. I hated talking about the six strokes, coma and brain surgery.

"How old were you when you had the strokes?" she asked.

"I'm forty-one. That was almost two years ago. I'm fully recovered." I was glad the coffee maker gave a final *blurp,* and a satisfied sigh. I poured three mugs of coffee, then set creamer, sugar and spoons on the table. Prentice sipped his coffee black and Midge sugared hers and then warmed her hands with the mug.

"Where are the searchers starting?" I asked.

"With our area first," Prentice said. "That's the logical way. The people Juliet knows. Most of us have security, so we know who goes in and out and what time. That's how we knew exactly when Juliet left the Du Pres house."

"At 11:42," Midge said.

"So how can I help?"

"Well, you're a Chouteau County ..." Midge stopped. "You investigate ... uh, you look into ... you work for ..."

Midge couldn't bring herself to say the two terrible words of my title, and Prentice didn't try.

"I'm a death investigator. I handle –"

Prentice cut me off before I could say "homicides."

"Yes, yes, we understand. But right now we need your contacts. You work with the Chouteau Forest detectives. The two best are Ray Foster Greiman and Butch Chetkin."

"They're certainly the most experienced." I thought Butch was the best and Greiman couldn't find sand in the Sahara, but I kept those opinions to myself.

"We need one of them to lead the search for Juliet," Prentice said. "The chief has called in the entire force, but he says Chetkin and Greiman are not available."

"Can't you talk to them?" Midge asked. "This is important." Her teary brown eyes were pleading. I was afraid she'd start crying again.

"Ray's out of town," I said, "and he doesn't answer his phone for anyone – not even the chief – when he's on vacation. Poor Butch has the flu. I doubt if he can stand up, much less lead an investigation."

"That means we're stuck with the new hire." Midge was not happy.

"What's wrong with Jason Budewitz?" I asked. "I haven't worked with him yet, but he comes highly recommended. He worked as a detective in Chicago."

"That's the problem," Midge said. "He's used to dealing with those people, not with our kind."

"Our kind?" I knew my kind definitely wasn't Midge's.

"She means Budewitz is used to dealing with a rougher element than we have here in the Forest," Prentice said. "Toonerville has some scruffy types, but not like the people he's encountered in Chicago."

"Dope dealers, prostitutes, killers and worse," Midge said.

"Then Detective Budewitz will appreciate working with nice, polite people even more," I said.

"That detective asked if Juliet had her tongue pierced! That's disgusting. What will people think if they find out he's asking questions like that?" I saw real fear in Midge's eyes, but I wasn't sure if it was for her lost daughter or her possibly lost reputation.

"People will know you're not asking that. They'll understand the police have to ask difficult questions.'"

The LaRouches looked doubtful. I tried to reassure them. "Mr. and Mrs. LaRouche, the detectives don't work for me. I work with them. We don't have the same bosses. I answer to the medical examiner, and their boss is the police chief. I don't have the power to influence the police or their schedules in any way. Is there anything else I can do?"

"Yes," Midge said. "We want to know if you remembered any teenagers tearing around on the roads here around midnight."

"No," I said. "I went to bed about ten and didn't hear anything. Did you check with the guard at the entrance to the estate?"

"He wasn't on duty last night," Prentice said, "but he said there were no reports of drag racing."

"Old Reggie has cracked down on that since his granddaughter was killed in a drag race on the estate," I said. "I promise I'll keep an eye out for Juliet. But I'm not sure what she looks like. Girls grow up so fast."

Midge pulled a photo out of her purse. "Here's her picture, the latest one, taken at the Holly Dance." The Holly Dance was the social event of the holiday season at the Chouteau Forest Academy.

Juliet was stunning, a rare ice blonde. Her straight, shoulder-length hair was so white it looked like moon glow. Her black velvet gown set off her pale skin and long, slender form. Her eyes were summer sky blue. Juliet stared at the camera with a hint of a smile. If Midge hadn't said her age, I would have guessed Juliet was a sophisticated twenty-one. I wondered how her hearty, ordinary-looking parents had created this delicate creature.

"Does Juliet have a boyfriend?" I asked.

"Absolutely not," her father said, as if that was a decree.

"Juliet told us that she's not really dating," Midge said. "She says dating is old school. She just hangs around with friends."

Friends. Right. One look at that picture and I knew Juliet was no wallflower. "Any of those friends boys?"

"I'm sure they are, but there's no one in particular," Prentice said. His wife nodded.

Her parents had bought Juliet's story. In my experience, teens didn't tell their parents everything, especially about their love lives.

"We wanted Detective Budewitz to put out an Amber Alert, but he said Juliet didn't meet the criteria because there was no proof she'd been abducted."

"He's right," I said. "Missouri has strict rules for Amber Alerts."

"Instead, he signed her up for a Missouri Endangered Persons Alert. That's useless." Midge's voice was warped with pain. She was crying again. Through her tears, she said, "All an Endangered Persons Alert does is let the police and the media know Juliet's missing. An Amber Alert has text messages that go to thousands of people, but an Endangered Persons Alert has nothing like that. What does it cost to put out a text alert for a missing girl who's not properly dressed for the freezing weather? We don't text much, but we know texting is how young people communicate. You know what this Budewitz advised? Posters! Posters in this day and age! How backward is that? Look at this stupid poster they did."

Midge opened her cell phone and there was a poster notice: "MISSING! SAVE ME! ENDANGERED PERSONS ALERT. Juliet LaRouche. Last seen December 26, 2017, 11:42 p.m."

Juliet, in her breathtaking black ball gown, smiled at the information about her last location: Chouteau Forest, Chouteau County, Missouri, her date of birth and other vital statistics, from her height to her hair color. "If you have any information on this child, call these numbers," the poster said, then listed numbers that could be contacted twenty-four hours a day.

I didn't know what to say. Midge was right. Posters were no match for a high-tech alert.

"We printed the posters at a twenty-four-hour copy shop," she said. "We're supposed to put these posters everywhere. The detective says they work."

"They do, Midge," I said. "They're your best chance."

Prentice squeezed his wife's shoulder. "She's right, old girl."

"Will you retweet the link to the poster and her photo?" Midge sounded lost.

"Of course." I gave the worried woman my contact information. Midge gave me the photo and texted me the poster, then glanced at the kitchen clock. "We should be going. It's almost seven. Thank you for your time, Angela."

"Would you like some coffee for the road?"

"No, no, we have a TV interview and a radio interview. Officer Budewitz thinks a personal plea from us will help, too." Midge zipped up her ski jacket, then slipped on her mittens.

"I'll do everything I can to help find Juliet," I said.

The couple carefully picked their way down the snow-slick concrete stairs, then trudged through the snow to their Range Rover. They seemed to be holding each other up.

As I watched them drive away, I wondered about their information. I thought Prentice was hiding something. He knew more about his daughter's disappearance than he was saying. He sounded defensive when he told me Juliet didn't date. And behind his fear was a deep undercurrent of anger. What fueled that? Juliet was dazzling. I couldn't believe the sixteen-year-old wasn't involved with a boy. Did she run away from her overly strict parents? Did her father know she was seeing someone unsuitable? Worse, was she suicidal? Teenagers had to deal with raging hormones. A disappointment in love at that age could be catastrophic.

I prayed the LaRouches' delicate snow princess was still alive. I had to find Juliet. I wasn't supposed to be investigating a missing person. That was Detective Budewitz's job. But he was new to the department, an outsider used to Chicago's mean streets, not the sly, subtle destructive ways of the wealthy Forest dwellers. I couldn't imagine what it must be like to lose a child. I'd had the heart-crushing experience of losing my husband, Donegan, two years ago. If I could help find Juliet, her parents wouldn't have to suffer that numbing, pointless grief. The last thing I wanted was to do my job – to examine Juliet's frozen body.

CHAPTER 2

Tuesday, December 27, 7:30 a.m.

The LaRouches nearly slipped on my snow-frosted porch on the way to their car. It needed to be cleared off before someone was hurt. Rick the handyman was due sometime this morning, but I wanted to get started in case I had more visitors before Rick arrived.

People always wanted the details of my strokes and coma, but I was sick of talking about them. I wanted to forget them. That's why I gave the LaRouches my standard line: I've made a full recovery after the strokes and brain surgery, but that's not quite true. I'm still not up to full strength, but I didn't want to sit in my kitchen jangling my nerves with more coffee. By the time I'd dressed in my warmest clothes, slipped the snow and ice grips on my boots, and dug the snow shovel out of the garage, I was sweating.

At first, stepping out into the cold felt good. The snowfall sparkled in the sun like spilled sugar, turning my white stone house into a storybook creation. But the frigid air slid down my throat and clutched my lungs. Even my nose hairs were frozen. That never happened in storybooks.

I brushed away the snow icing on the white wooden railing of my gingerbread porch and slid slightly. Gripping the railing with one hand, I pushed the snow off the flat porch. Soon my fingers were numb and so was my nose. My lungs hurt from the cold. Under the first layer of soft snow was ice, and now the porch was even slipperier. I needed rock salt. How was I going to drag a fifty-pound bag out of the garage?

Quit being such a wuss, I told myself. Pour some salt into a bucket and get on with it. I was still holding the shovel when the Forest's hippie handyman, Rick DeMun, rumbled up my gravel drive in an ancient pickup with a snow plow attachment.

He cranked down the window, and I swore I saw clouds of pot smoke waft out. "Angela! Why didn't you wait for me? Here, let me do that."

He jumped out of his truck, his vintage brown suede fur-lined ranch coat flapping around his legs, its fur-lined hood and a peace sign balaclava protecting his face, and ran for the back of his truck.

"Cool coat." My voice was muffled by the wool scarf wrapped around my mouth. "Where did you get it?"

"Etsy," he said. "Summer of love – 1968."

I knew he longed to return to that enchanted time. He pulled a snow shovel out of the back of his truck, along with a bucket of rock salt.

"Here," he said, taking the shovel out of my hands and propping it against my door. "Let me finish this." He put some muscle behind his ice-chopping, shoveling, and scraping as he cleared the porch, moving surprisingly fast for someone wearing so many layers of clothes. I watched him shovel from a sunny corner of my porch. He worked at a steady rhythm.

Rick was a renegade rich kid, a Forest insider who was a successful local contractor.. In the winter, he also removed ice and snow. Rick's hard-charging parents were puzzled that they'd raised a gentle pothead who worked at his own pace. The rest of the Forest rejoiced: he was reasonable, reliable, and resourceful when he fixed their ancient plumbing and drafty old buildings.

When he finished the porch and started on the steps, Rick was panting slightly. "I had to clear Old Man Du Pres's drive first," he said, "and I was slowed down by the searchers. You know Juliet LaRouche is missing?"

"Her poor parents were here at six-thirty this morning asking if I knew where she was. They're worried sick. They think she got lost on the path to her house."

Rick stopped for a second and looked at me. "If she's really lost in the woods, they should be scared. How are they ever going to find her? Have you looked at this place – I mean really looked?" His arm swept the sun-dazzled scenery, where parties of searchers trudged through the snowy fields and poked at the snow-burdened brush at the edge of the woods.

"Every estate is wooded and has little creeks and streams that flood in the spring, then turn into dry gullies. There are limestone outcroppings, and so many caves, ditches and sinkholes I can't count them. Her body could have fallen into one of them and been covered by the snow. If that happens, she won't be found until spring."

"Please don't say 'body.' I'm on call today, Rick. I don't want to investigate her death. I'm hoping she's still alive."

"My little sister Daisy thinks she is." Rick was shoveling the top layer of snow off the steps with swift, sure strokes. *Shovel, shovel, crunch. Shovel, shovel, crunch.* "Daisy was at the party last night. She thinks Juliet's hiding at somebody's house."

"Really?" I felt a warm surge of hope. "Your sister knows Juliet?"

"They're buds. It's 'Juliet this …' and 'Juliet that …'"

My teeth were chattering so much I could hardly get the words out. "Will your sister talk to me?" Weird. My speech sounded slurred, like I'd been drinking.

"Angela, you're shaking so bad you can't even talk. That's hypothermia. Get inside."

"But –"

"Now! It's seven below." He hopped up the stairs, took my arm, and opened my front door. "Inside." He gave me a slight push. "You're not dressed for this weather. That wool hat isn't warm enough. Another sign of hypothermia is clumsiness. You can't risk a fall. Go in, warm up, and make me some hot coffee. I'll finish the sidewalk and come in for a cup before I do your driveway."

"But I need to know about Daisy."

"And I'll tell you on my coffee break. *Make me coffee, woman.*"

Rick's mock command made me laugh.

Once inside, I realized Rick was right – something was wrong. I was still shivering, but my heart was pounding. I felt dizzy and clumsy. I picked my way carefully across my living room and plopped down in a kitchen chair. After sitting a while, I felt a little better. If I felt like this after being outside for what – I glanced at the clock – twenty minutes – how could Juliet survive a walk home in ten below weather wearing only a light jacket, a strapless dress, and heels?

I hoped Rick's sister was right and Juliet was hiding with her friends. But why would a girl her parents said was so good do that?

I knew that answer, too. As a death investigator, I learned the dead had many secrets: good husbands had long-running affairs and good wives had gambling habits. I remembered the Forest suicide who'd secretly maxed out her credit cards and gambled away her home's equity on the St. Louis river boats, then killed herself when she ran out of money. And teens? They lied about everything: their boyfriends and girlfriends, drugs, money, you name it. Maybe Juliet had a Romeo she didn't want her parents to know about, and she was sleeping in his bed while Mummy and Daddy skied at Telluride. I hoped so.

I could hear Rick shoveling my sidewalk. My heart rate had slowed to nearly normal, and I didn't feel dizzy. I poured out the sludge I'd made for the LaRouches and made fresh coffee. Then I found a loaf of banana bread in the freezer and warmed it in the microwave. Now I could hear the dull ping of rock salt hitting concrete.

By the time Rick was stamping the snow off his boots in the mud room, I had hot coffee and warm banana bread on the table. He came into the kitchen, bringing the cold and his cannabis cologne with him. He was wearing a hairy sweater over an insulated undershirt. He sniffed the coffee-scented air, then looked at the loaf on the plate. "Is that banana bread?"

I handed him the butter. "It is. Eat up and get warm, then tell me about Daisy and Juliet."

Rick gulped his coffee, slathered the banana bread with thick slabs of butter, and two slices later said, "How come you're interested in Juliet? I thought you only worked on dead people."

"I do. And I don't want to have to investigate Juliet's death. I'm not supposed to investigate her disappearance at all. It's not my job, not my department. I'm sticking my nose in a police investigation. If it was another detective," I didn't mention Greiman's name, "I wouldn't trespass. He'd shut me down and report me to the ME. I'm hoping the new guy won't mind my help. The last thing I want is a dead girl during holidays – or any time, for that matter."

"That's cool." He cut himself a third slice. I poured more coffee.

"Besides, I talked with her parents," I said. "Those poor people. They're frantic. Once I saw their faces, I had to do something. Do you think Daisy will talk to me?"

Rick thoughtfully chewed his buttered banana bread, then said, "She might, but she'd be more likely to talk if you did her a favor. Daisy's not like me. She's, uh … practical."

"Can I pay her?"

Rick laughed. "She's not that mercenary. It's not like she's a hooker or anything."

I blushed.

"She's more into something for something. Her car's in the shop and she wants to hang with her friends. I'd drive her, but Mother thinks I'm a bad influence. She won't lend Daisy her car, but she offered to drive her. Daisy would curl up and die before she'd be seen with Mother. But you, you've got a cool car."

"I remember being like that. Which mall does she go to?"

"Mall?" Rick took a long drink of coffee. "Kids don't go to malls much anymore. Sadly, these kids hang out at the Show Me gas station mini mart. Freaks me out."

"A gas station? What do they do there?"

"They vape, smoke, drink Polar cup refills, and meet up with their friends. Occasionally some pot gets sold on the back lot."

"I hate to sound like my grandmother, but kids nowadays …"

"I know," Rick said. "They also hang at houses with the kind of parents who want to be *friends* with their kids. I did that because I like weed, but Daisy doesn't partake. Daisy and her buds hang at the new Olive Garden."

I paused, the cup halfway to my mouth. "The Olive Garden? Do they bring two-for-one coupons?"

"Now, now." Rick grinned at me. "They love those all-you-can-eat bread sticks. I'll tell Daisy you're not bad for a grownup. It may take her a while to warm up to you, but she's dying to go to the Olive Garden."

"Aren't all her friends looking for Juliet?"

"Most of them, yeah. But unlike other Forest kids, Daisy hangs with kids from other schools in West County, too."

West County. The rich part of St. Louis County. "Like Parkway?"

Rick looked embarrassed. "More like MICDS." Mary Institute and St. Louis Country Day. The rich kids' private school. Parkway was a public school district.

"The drive will give us time to talk."

"She wants to go today, if you have time. Can you take her if you're on call?"

"I don't have to go into the office. All I have to do is be available when the office calls. If there's a death investigation, Daisy would just have to spend more time with her friends."

"She'd like that. She'll do anything to get out – even talk to a grownup."

"Deal. Tell me when and where."

Rick checked the kitchen clock. "She's still snoozing. I'll wait till after nine to text her." He stood up. "Meanwhile, I'll salt your drive and send you a bill. If Daisy says yes, you know where our house is?"

"Du Champ Road. Second house on the right."

"That's it." He gulped the rest of his coffee. "Well, back to the salt mines – or the salt, anyway. Thanks for the coffee and banana bread."

I tidied the kitchen, then sat on the leather living room couch, cell phone at my side. I meant to go through the bills, but I drifted off to sleep until I heard the *ping* of an incoming text from Rick: *Daisy's itching to go. Pick her up at 11.*

Rick sent this warning: *Remember, Daisy's a little spoiled. She's not a bad kid, but you gotta be firm with her.*

CHAPTER 3

Tuesday, December 27, 10:54 a.m.

As I drove to Du Champ Road, I watched teenagers in bulky coats, boots, and dark green Chouteau Forest Academy scarves and hats search the ditches along the Forest's snowy, landscaped streets.

"Juliet!" they called, their shrill voices echoing in the cold. "Juliet!"

The snow muffled their cries and froze their hopes, but the students never stopped calling and searching. Occasionally someone would throw a snowball – the snow was just right, it packed well – but attempts to play were quickly quashed. They were on a mission and time was short. They had to rescue the ice princess.

How long could they keep searching for the girl in this bone-chilling freeze? It looked like the whole Academy had turned out to look for Juliet. Everyone except her good friend Daisy. Why didn't she say something if she knew where Juliet was?

Most of the Forest roads had been plowed and salted. An army of county plows were unleashed when the first snowflake hit the pavement, and contractors rolled out to clear the private streets and drives. Driving was fairly easy as long as I kept an eye out for slick spots. I turned onto

Du Champ Road and the DeMun house rose like a white cloud above the bare-branched trees, its graceful marble tamed into creamy curves, its shiny black lacquered doors flanked by topiary trees.

Before I pulled up at the front door, a teenage girl slouched out in a long red hooded coat and knee-high black suede boots. I stopped my black Dodge Charger, and Daisy slid into the black bucket seat, bringing a frosty rush of air.

"Hi, I'm Angela Richman." I turned up the heater.

"Hi." That word was a massive effort, a boulder Daisy had rolled uphill.

"So you want to go to Olive Garden?"

Daisy nodded, and I wondered if saying "yes" would be too tiring. Rick's little sister looked nothing like her brother. She was pretty, but she wasn't an ethereal beauty like her missing friend. Daisy was slim with straw-colored hair and brown eyes. Her delicate complexion was marred by a slight sneer.

"You got any music?" Four whole words.

"Sure, a case of CDs in the back seat."

Daisy reached back to retrieve the case, flipped through my CD collection, and delivered her verdict. "Mom music."

That was an insult. "Do you want to listen to the radio?"

"The radio?" Daisy's voice was etched in acid. "Don't you have any playlists Bluetoothed to your car?"

"No."

"That's how everyone does music." Daisy sighed, a queen captured by a barbarian. She dumped the CD case in the back, jewel boxes spilling over the foot well, then flopped back into her seat, folded her arms, and plugged in the earbuds she'd produced from her purse. She would endure the next twenty minutes listening to her own tunes.

I panicked. How could I learn anything about Juliet from my silent, surly passenger? I remembered Rick's advice: *She's not a bad kid, but you gotta be firm with her.*

We were on Gravois Road now, the main thoroughfare through the town of Chouteau Forest. More searchers combed the roadsides and the woods in pairs, their calls for Juliet sounding like sad birds. Daisy stared out the window, looking past them. I had almost reached the highway. Time to learn anything was running out.

"Hey!"

Now I had Daisy's attention. "Why aren't you searching for Juliet? Don't you care that she may have frozen to death?" I steered the black Charger carefully, driving slower than usual in this treacherous section, with impatient drivers zipping around me. We were in the Forest business district, passing gas stations, pizza places, and specialty food stores.

"Juliet isn't dead. I'd know." A positive torrent of speech.

"So where is she?"

"Probably hiding at the Minterns' house. At Christmas, the Minterns go away for two weeks to Abaco, and they take Trey with them."

"Trey?"

"He's one of us. Goes to the Academy. We all have the code to get into his house. Right now, we hang at his house and he's cool with it, but we have to be careful. If someone makes a mess, we'll get caught. We use a lot of houses like that during the winter."

So Juliet was safe at the Minterns' house. I relaxed a little. The girl would be in trouble when her parents found out, but she was alive.

"Won't Juliet freeze with no heat in the Minterns' house?"

"They have to keep some heat on or the pipes will freeze." Daisy's tone made me feel like a slow learner. "Her boyfriend probably took her there."

A semi shouldered past me, splattering my black car with oily slush. I slowed down while the wipers cleaned the window. "Her parents said Juliet didn't have a boyfriend."

Daisy snorted. I guessed the girl rolled her eyes but didn't dare take my eyes off this slippery part of the road.

"They don't know anything." Daisy's scorn could have melted the roadside snow piles. I decided Daisy wasn't going to the Olive Garden after all. I made a U-turn on Gravois Road, narrowly missing an oncoming car. The irate driver hit the horn as Daisy shrieked, "Hey! What are you doing? The Olive Garden is the other way!"

"And the Minterns' house is this way. You're not pigging out on bread sticks while the whole Forest searches for Juliet. You're not doing that to her parents."

"They'll get over it."

"No, they won't." I checked my dashboard clock. Top of the hour. TV would have a news update. I moved over to the side of the road, pulled my iPad from the neoprene case that kept it warm in the cold weather, and called up the local TV station's website. Sure enough, Juliet's disappearance was the main story. "Watch this," I said, and held the iPad so we both could see it.

Onscreen, a haggard, red-eyed Midge LaRouche was pleading: "Please, if you know where my little girl is, please help. Time is running out."

I saw – and heard – the tears in Juliet's mother's voice. Daisy stared at the video stone-faced, then stuck in her ear buds as I threaded the Charger through the traffic.

"Hey, Daisy. Didn't you see that video? That was Juliet's mother and she's frantic with worry. Take those things out of your ears! Now! We're going to the Minterns' house and you're going to let me in."

"No! You're kidnapping me. I'm calling the police." She waved her cell phone like a weapon.

"Go ahead. I'll tell them you think she's at the Minterns' house. They'll break down the door and you and your friends will be busted – no more holiday hideout. It's your pick: the cops check the Minterns' or we do. And while we're driving there, you're going to tell me about this boyfriend. Who is he?"

A sullen silence. Then, "Some dickhead named Dex – I think it's short for Dexter – Gordon. His dad's a mechanic. Owns a shop. In Toonerville."

"How did she meet him?"

Daisy twisted a hunk of dirty-blonde hair. Her pale face was pink with anger. "Her father took his car there. Shop's called Gordon's Repairs and Restorations. It's cheaper than the Beemer dealer, but her daddy's paying big-time now. She's fucking that little nobody."

"Is Dex handsome?"

Daisy shrugged. "If you like greasers. Her parents hate him, so she has to sneak out to see him."

My car hit a pothole, then slid slightly on a patch of ice. I steered into the skid and the car righted itself. Daisy paled and gripped the door handle.

"What's wrong with Dex, except that his father is a mechanic?" I was on a cleared road again, and the ride was smoother.

"Isn't that enough? Juliet's mother is always lecturing her to meet 'suitable young men.'" Daisy made those last three words singsong.

"What's that mean? Smart? Interesting?"

"Rich and well-connected." The girl sounded world-weary, sixteen going on sixty. "You know. The so-called Forest first families. Juliet's mother has big plans for her. Her father's given a shitload of money so when she turns eighteen Juliet can be Queen of the Daughters of Versailles Ball. Juliet doesn't give two shits about being a DV Queen, but her mother's nuts on the subject."

"Why does Midge care? Don't most debs think the DV Ball is boring?"

"Yeah, it's like so 1950. More like 1850. But Juliet's mother scored big at her DV debut. My mom says her family has a good name but no money, and Prentice LaRouche is loaded. Well, kinda loaded. Bella's family is richer."

Bella. I assumed she was the cousin who had the party. "Prentice isn't exactly standing in the welfare line. He has his own jet."

"It's only a Mustang. He's cheaping out because it only needs one pilot. Most jets have two. Mrs. L. wants Juliet to date the right boys. Juliet thinks they're boring. She likes Dex's car, too. It's not one more Beemer."

What kind of world do you live in, I wondered, where you're bored with Beemers at sixteen?

"What's Dex drive?"

"A sixty-eight tangerine orange GTO. It's like vintage. He restored it himself. Dex can't pick her up at her house, and his car makes it hard for Juliet to sneak out and be with him – it's like the only one in the Forest and the muffler's noisy."

"So how does Juliet sneak away?"

"She takes the path through the woods that runs around the back of her house. It's only about half a block to her house on the path, but you can't see it from the street because there are so many trees. It comes out by the stop sign that leads to her street. Dex picks up Juliet by that sign and her parents never know."

"Why is she hiding out so long this time?"

"To get away from her parents? Get them off her case? She needed time away and I'm not going to interfere."

"Even if the whole Forest is looking for her?"

Daisy shrugged. "They love it. Makes them feel like heroes."

I had reached the residential part of Chouteau Forest again. "How far to the Minterns' house from here?"

"Next right. Third house on the left."

As I turned off Gravois, I saw groups of Boy Scouts searching the nearby woods. Someone had set up a tent with hot drinks. A police car with lights flashing was parked nearby. The wind had picked up, and the snow was drifting. I prayed Juliet was in the Minterns' house.

"Most of us don't really like Dex," Daisy said. "We don't understand why she's in love with him. But we like her, and she's crazy about him, so he tags along."

We passed the first estate, and I saw cameras bristling on the curli-cued wrought-iron gates. "What kind of security do the Minterns have – besides the alarm code?"

"Cameras."

"How do you get past them?"

"Dex hit them with water in a spray bottle. Iced the lenses. Frozen over lenses happen all the time in cold weather, so the security company doesn't come rushing out."

"Clever."

Daisy wouldn't even give Dex that. "At least he's good for something."

"Then we're definitely going in."

"Can't we wait?"

"Not another minute," I said.

CHAPTER 4

Tuesday, December 27, 11:25 a.m.

In the mid-1950s, Russell Jedidiah Mintern did the unthinkable: he tore down his family's Victorian castle. The ancestor-worshipping Forest dwellers were shocked. But that shock turned to envy when they heard about Mintern's greatly reduced heating bills and smaller household staff – not to mention his efficient air-conditioning during the sweltering Missouri summers. No first family would do that to their family houses, but the Mintern house was an interesting experiment.

I liked the clean lines of the brick and redwood Mintern estate. The "new" house was huge by any standard – three cantilevered stories jutted in different directions. Wide windows let in the light and sun. Beyond the gates, the drive curved into the thickly wooded area that sheltered the house.

"Oh, good," I said. "The driveway's been shoveled. My car won't leave tracks in the snow."

Daisy kept her sullen silence. I stopped at the gate entrance and Daisy punched the code into the keypad. The gates swung open and

I followed the twisting drive around to the back of the house. There, my heart dropped in disappointment. "No cars." I was afraid to add, *Juliet isn't here.*

"Well, duh," Daisy said. "We're not dumb enough to park our cars on the property. We'd get caught. We come in through the back fence. If you follow that path through the woods, there's a hole in the chain-link that we sorta fixed."

"Fixed?"

"Made it wider so we could squeeze through. It was snagging our clothes. There's an old floor mat in a tree limb that we use to protect us when the ground's muddy."

Daisy pointed to the path, and I saw the snow had been trampled. A good sign. Juliet was inside, and soon she'd be reunited with her family.

"We go in on the garden level." Daisy was whispering. I hoped the girl was keeping her voice low so she wouldn't disturb Juliet. I followed Daisy down rough stone steps to a sunken garden, now shrouded in snow. The stairs were treacherous. The steps had been shoveled and salted, but they were still slick with ice. I hung onto the railing. Daisy had skipped ahead. "Hurry up!" she called. "I'm freezing, and I can't punch in the code until you get here. We only have ninety seconds to get in."

I finally reached the garden level door. Daisy wiped her feet on the mat, then punched in the code. "Take your boots off and leave them on the rug," she whispered.

The warm, humid air smothered me, and my hair frizzed and hung in my face. The garden level was a jungle of palms, from small, bushy cabbage palms to twenty-foot date palms. Green vines twisted up trellises to grow lights in the ceiling. Purple orchids bloomed in hanging baskets. I heard a fountain splashing. I was sweating. I unbuttoned my coat and followed Daisy on a wet concrete path through the steamy jungle and out into a vast, open room with a stone fireplace and groups of mid-century modern furniture. The closest was a low red couch, two acid yellow side chairs, and a scattering of egg-shaped sculptures.

Daisy picked a roach out of the fireplace and held it up. "See. This is what I mean. Some idiot was toking and left this." She put the joint in her purse. "And here's a Bud Light can. What's wrong with these people? They're going to ruin everything."

She emptied the dregs of the beer can into the fireplace, then stuck that in her purse, too. Daisy plumped the couch pillows, mumbling to herself.

"Daisy, we don't have time to clean the house. Where's Juliet?"

"Well, we sort of hang on this level, mostly in this room."

I pointed to three closed doors. "What about those?"

"You can check them, but I don't think she's inside."

The first door led to a laundry room. I was sure Juliet wasn't hiding in there. She wasn't in the utilities room either. The food storage room looked like it had been ravaged by raccoons; crumpled packages of Oreo cookies and snack boxes were strewn on the floor. Empty chip and Doritos bags littered the floor along with snack food wrappers.

"Daisy, have you seen this?"

Daisy burst into a string of curses. "Those stupid fuckers. It's bad enough they cleaned out the snacks, but they trashed the room, too. Assholes!" She started gathering the packages, but I stopped her. "Later! We need to find Juliet."

I followed Daisy up to the next level, a dazzling display of colorful 1950s furniture with the classic shapes: a boomerang coffee table, lamps shaped like nuclear reactors, sleek oval chairs, a kidney-shaped couch, and a bronze sculpture of an abstract female figure that I thought might be a Henry Moore.

Daisy surveyed the room and said, "Thank gawd they weren't here. Last time, somebody left a go-cup on that statue."

I followed the girl through a maze of bedrooms. One bed looked like it had been slept in, and I felt a flash of hope. "Do you think Juliet slept in this room?"

"Doubt it." Daisy picked a gym sock off the floor and said, "That's rank. Ew!" She ran into a bathroom, wrapped the offending – and offensive – sock in toilet paper, and stashed it in her now bulging purse.

I wouldn't let her stop to remake the bed. "We're looking for Juliet, remember?"

Daisy whined and I said, "At least you get to search for her in a nice warm house instead of the freezing woods."

We checked the kitchen last. The lime Formica counters were sticky with soda, and crumbs littered the round table. "I have to clean those. They'll draw bugs." I helped Daisy wipe down the counters and table top, then said, "That's the whole house. She's not here. Where's Juliet?"

I was interrogating the girl in the breakfast room under a 1950s Sputnik star-burst lamp that looked like a metal spider.

Daisy's eyes glittered in the light and her damp hair was wild. "I know she's not dead." Her voice had lost some of its confidence.

"Then she's alive. Whose house was she at last night?"

"I told you, Bella's. She had to invite Dex to her party and she didn't want to, but Juliet cried and made her."

"That's her cousin, right? Is she related to Old Reggie Du Pres?"

"Yes, they're all related, but I'm not sure how. My mom pays attention to that." Daisy's pale face was sullen and her nose was shiny. She sniffled and I wondered if she was crying for her lost friend or getting a cold. "Can't we go to the Olive Garden now? Please? You promised."

"I also promised Juliet's parents that I'd find their daughter, and that promise comes first. The sooner we find Juliet the sooner you can go to the Olive Garden."

Daisy made a move to stand up, and I blocked her. "Sit! And tell me about this party." Overhead, the shining, spidery lamp seemed ready to pounce.

Daisy sat. "Bella had it at her house. Her parents are cool. They let us party and went upstairs and shut the door to their room and we could do like anything."

"Drink?"

"Of course we drank. And had a DJ, and more. Dex and Juliet had a fight."

"What did they fight about?"

"You'd have to ask Bella."

"I will. I want to talk to her now."

"She's at home."

"Then we'll go there."

"No!" Daisy stood up again.

"Sit down!" I said. "You're miles from your house. There's no way you can walk home in this cold. Text Bella that you need to see her now."

"Can we go to the Olive Garden?"

"What the hell's wrong with you? It's one o'clock. Juliet has been missing for more than thirteen hours. If she's outside, she's frozen like a pork chop."

Daisy started to cry. "You're mean. You didn't have to say that."

I tried to feel bad, but I couldn't. Reality was cold – even colder than the deep-freeze weather. I softened my voice. "I'm sorry you're upset, Daisy. But this isn't a game. If you want to save Juliet, we're wasting time. Please text Bella. We'll talk in my car."

"What if she doesn't want to talk?" Daisy sniffled.

"She'll talk." I tried to smooth the snarl out of my voice. "Or I'll tell my cop friends that her parents were serving liquor to minors."

"So? Happens all the time." Daisy was defiant – and right. The Forest police went out of their way to protect and serve the one percent.

They not only overlooked drunken underage drivers, they helped park cars for the parties.

"Maybe it does, but this time one of those minors disappeared in ten below weather. If the cops aren't worried about a teen booze party – though I think they will be – there's always TV. The St. Louis stations are covering Juliet's disappearance and they'll go nuts with that information."

"That's so uncool." Daisy meant that barb to hurt, but it bounced off my hide. Juliet was missing, and I didn't care how many toes I stepped on to find her.

"Uncool? So is having cops and reporters at Bella's house. Text her that I'm on my way and explain why she'd better talk."

The text *ping* was back two minutes later. "She'll do it, but she doesn't want us to come up her driveway. She's got a cough and she's not supposed to go outside. She'll take the path and meet us before we get to her gate."

Two minutes later, I was carefully climbing the Minterns' stone steps to my car. The temperature was dropping. A harsh wind blew snow across the newly shoveled steps. Daisy frowned down at me from the top of the stairs. "Come on. I'm freezing. Open your car."

I had no sympathy for the girl. "So is Juliet if she's outside. Let's hope she's not frozen." I chirped open my car.

"You're awful. I'm glad Bella only lives two houses away. Less time with you."

Fine with me, I thought, but decided not to provoke the girl. Back in the Charger, I blasted the heat and defogged the windows. As I turned left out of the Mintern driveway, I saw lines of bundled up adults, moving like Michelin men through the woods around Bella's house, and wondered if they were doing a grid search.

"Stop!" Daisy shouted. "That's Bella."

The clipped yew bushes by the roadside parted and a short, sturdy, brown-haired girl in a long dark green coat hurried to the car. Daisy crawled into the back seat so her friend could sit up front. Bella greeted us with a hacking cough. She smelled like menthol cough drops.

"I shouldn't–" *hack, hack* "–be out of bed." *Wheeze.*

I thought the girl was overdoing it. I didn't see any signs of a bad cold – no watery eyes or red, runny nose, no fever flush. Bella clutched a tissue in her mittened paw but didn't use it.

"You can go back home as soon as you give me the information I need."

Sigh. "Okay." Bella gave that word four syllables. "What do you want?"

"Tell me about Dex Gordon."

"He was Juliet's first." *Hack, hack.* "She made a big deal out of it. I don't see the issue over a piece of tissue, but she wanted her first to be special. Dex didn't seem all that special to me, but he was to her." *Hack, hack.* "At the party, I heard him bragging about 'putting it to her' and I thought Juliet should know." *Hack, hack.* "So I told her. It's always better to know the truth." *Hack, hack.*

You little witch, I thought. "How did Juliet take it?"

"I was careful when I told her. She'd been playing beer pong, and she was drunk. She got drunk pretty quick. She weighs like a hundred-fifteen pounds. She doesn't really like beer anyway. She just drank it because of the game. She got tired of beer and found some Grey Goose in my parents' liquor cabinet. She poured some into her water bottle and drank that, too. She was *not* having a good time. Besides Dex, she'd already had some kind of fight with Brock."

"Brock who?" I asked.

"Brock Sedgwick," Bella said, as if I was too stupid to understand. Another Forest first family.

"What about?"

She shrugged. "He's wanted to do her for a long time. See if she's really blonde *down there*. He's really pissed she puts out for a Toonerville nobody. She told him no again. I've never seen him so angry. He called her a slut, and then he punched the wall so hard his knuckles were bloody. So Brock upset her. Mom was down in the kitchen getting herself a snack. She came the back way so she wouldn't bother us. She said something and that got Juliet crying and stuff. Mom calmed her down and gave her some kinda present or something, but Juliet was still upset. And the Dex thing was like the last straw. I made sure she'd had a few before I told her. I'm not like cruel or anything."

Right. Now that Bella was telling her story, I noticed her cough had vanished.

"She didn't believe me, so I told her the details. Dex had laughed at her and said that Juliet thought this was true love, when all he wanted was a fuck. He said rich girls didn't screw as well as poor ones. He laughed about her small tits."

I tried to control my fury. Bella was a nasty little creature, and plain by Forest standards. Chunky Bella had the kind of short, muscular body that would be good at sports. But I was sure Bella didn't want that skill.

"And how did Juliet take that news?" I asked.

"She got kinda hysterical. She said Dex was the only boy she'd ever loved and if he treated her that way, she'd kill herself."

"You don't think she would, do you?"

"Of course not." Bella was scornful. "She's such a drama queen. People who talk about suicide never do it."

"Not true," I said.

Daisy jumped into the conversation from the back seat. "She never said anything about suicide to me. I offered to drive her home, but Juliet wanted to confront Dex. She was sure he'd never say anything so mean. They drove off in his car a little before midnight."

"At 11:42," I said.

"How do you know?" Bella asked.

"Her parents told me. They got the time from your security."

"Okay. She left before midnight in Dex's car. Before the snow started. Can I go home now?"

My phone gave the special alert. Both girls jumped. "Jesus! What's that?" Daisy said.

I checked the text. "You're in luck, girls. There's a car accident on Gravois Road. The medical examiner's office wants me to go to work."

"Is someone dead?" Daisy asked in a small voice.

"Yes."

"Is it … is it Juliet?"

"I don't know." I caught Daisy's flour-white face in the rearview mirror. It had finally dawned on the girl: death was real. It could even strike someone in their enchanted circle.

CHAPTER 5

Tuesday, December 27, 3:44 p.m.

All the way to the accident scene, I prayed that Juliet wasn't dead. Why didn't I ask if the victim was a man or a woman?

Because I was in a hurry. And I wanted rid of those obnoxious girls.

Well, I'd find out soon enough. I could see the flashing emergency lights ahead on Gravois Road. Red flares burned a warning along the snow-piled road, and traffic slowed to a crawl. An impatient silver Mercedes in front of me shot out of the waiting line to pass the accident scene. The driver lost control when he hit a slick spot and his shiny new car slid into a ditch.

I held my breath.

Please don't make this a double death scene, I thought. The cars ahead of me didn't move and neither did the Mercedes, now with a demolished front end. At last, the driver emerged from his wrecked car, so shaky he held onto the door frame. He was greeted by a uniform who calmly wrote a series of tickets.

I was close enough now to see the death investigation site, but that car was hidden by a white folding privacy screen. All I could make out was a broken maple tree atop a black car. A red ambulance was parked off to the side, lights flashing. Did that mean there were survivors? I hoped so.

I waved to the uniform at the scene, pulled over and parked on the shoulder. I opened my iPad – the Forest had great WiFi – and called up two forms: Death Scene Investigation and Vehicular Related Death, then pulled up my hood, tucked my wool scarf up to my eyes, and pushed out of my car into the searing cold. I dragged my death investigator suitcase out of the car trunk and rolled it toward the scene. A uniform rushed forward to help, but I stopped him. "Thanks, Jim. I can handle it."

Now I could see the accident clearly: A black Lexus had crashed into a huge maple, cracking the tree trunk. The raw wood was exposed, and bare, broken branches speared the car's front end. The Lexus was smashed almost to the shattered windshield. I still couldn't tell where the driver was. In the ambulance?

Detective Jason "Jace" Budewitz, the new hire, was working the fatal accident. He was a muscular six feet two, made bigger by a bulky gray hooded parka lined in fake fur. His short blond hair revealed lots of cold-reddened scalp. He had an open, almost boyish face.

"Angela!" he said.

I could see his breath. "Is she dead?"

"She? The victim's a man." Jace had a distinct Chicago accent. His accent was even more nasal than ours, and he spoke faster than we did

Then Juliet was alive – the girl hadn't been driving the wrecked Lexus. Ashamed of my unprofessional reaction, I tried to hide my relief. A man is dead, I reminded myself. "Who is it? What happened?"

"The wit – she's over there with the paramedics – saw it happen. She's part of a group searching for the missing girl. She was walking along this side of Gravois when she saw the Lexus coming straight at her. She dove into the ditch, and the car roared past and slammed into the tree. *Wham!* Guy musta been doing a hundred when he took out the tree. Didn't even try to stop. Two men in the search party pulled the wit out of the ditch and someone called 911."

"Suicide?"

"Looks like it. No skid marks, his foot's on the gas pedal, and his hands are gripping the steering wheel. We're gonna have to pry his fingers off."

"What about his air bag?"

"Never deployed. Either he wasn't wearing a seat belt or it failed. We'll check that out later."

I could see the paramedics comforting the witness, a thin, weeping woman shivering in a blanket, while uniforms kept back a crowd of curious searchers.

"Was the witness injured?"

"Couple of scratches. Nothing serious, but she's in shock. She identified the dead guy as her neighbor Delano Corbet. Says this is his car and his license and registration confirm that. License says he's fifty-six years old and the address matches the one the neighbor lady gave us. She plays bridge with his wife, Iris. She's known the victim for twenty-five years."

"At least his wife won't have to ID him," I said.

"I'm not sure the ME would let her, the shape he's in."

When victims are badly decomposed or injured, the ME often uses dental records to ID them. Sometimes family members insist on seeing their loved one. In that case, I have to explain the possible trauma they risk. I urge them to remember the dead person as they'd knew him. Some still insist on viewing the body, saying they need closure. In that case, the family member has to sign a paper absolving the ME's office from any legal consequences.

"Brace yourself," Jace said. "It's bad."

I could see the upper part of Corbet's body through the broken side window. The victim's bloody head and shoulders were on the dashboard, surrounded by pebbles of red-tinted safety glass.

"The paramedics pronounced him dead at the scene at –" Jace checked his notebook – "3:17 p.m."

"Did they try to resuscitate him?"

"One look and they knew he was a no-hoper."

I wrote on my form that Corbet's car was a black Lexus IS 250 with Missouri plates, a medium-priced luxury car. I photographed the death scene: first a wide shot, then a medium, and finally a close up. I noted the time – 3:49 p.m. – and the weather conditions: sunny daylight, wind out of the northeast, temperature minus six degrees. Definitely getting colder. The car was heading westbound on Gravois Road, and the speed limit was forty. The road was straight, the roadway cleared of snow and ice, and there was no glare from the setting sun to blind the driver. Nothing natural caused this accident.

A frigid wind tore at my face. I pulled my hood tighter and tried to ignore it. My gloved fingers ached from the cold already.

Corbet was in the driver's seat, black, leafless branches grabbing his gory head. The back of his black wool topcoat was drenched in blood. I started the body actualization, working from the top. Corbet would have to be moved for me to finish.

His head was slightly turned toward the right. I measured the wounds on the back of his bloody head: Corbet had a deep eight-inch gash (officially a cut-like defect) at his crown – almost to the parietal bone. A tree branch with a half-inch circumference had pierced his right eye. I shuddered at the wound and forced myself to continue documenting. There was a two-inch cut-like defect on his right cheek over the temporal bone. I photographed and measured the blood from those wounds, then noted the eighteen superficial cut-like defects on his right cheek and neck, all less than half an inch long. I guessed those were from the tree branches and the broken windshield, but it wasn't my job to speculate. I photographed the broken twigs, dead leaves, and glass pebbles on his head and shoulders, then tweezered them off and bagged them.

Corbet wore a black wool topcoat, blue wool scarf, and black leather driving gloves. I saw a Cartier tank watch on his left wrist and recorded it as "a yellow metal watch with a rectangular face, worn brown leather strap, brand name Cartier." He also had "oval yellow metal cuff links with the initials DAC." I didn't know if he was wearing a wedding ring. The medical examiner would remove his gloves.

Corbet's blood-soaked hair was gray and thinning at the crown. His bald spot made him look vulnerable. Along with the coppery odor of blood, I caught the strong stink of liquor. On the floor of the passenger side foot well was a nearly empty bottle of Laphroaig single malt scotch.

"The man went out with the best," the detective said.

I noted the liquor odor and photographed the scotch bottle. The ME would check his blood alcohol level.

"That's all I can do with him in the car. Can we move him, detective?"

"We're ready," Jace said. He laid out a black body bag on the frozen ground. I removed a sterilized sheet from a plastic bag in my suitcase and spread it on top of the open body bag. A paramedic cut the tree branch in the Corbet's eye about three inches from his face and left it in place. I covered the branch with a paper bag and secured it with string. Then the paramedics pried Corbet's fingers off the steering wheel and placed the dead man on the sheet. I measured his height at five feet eleven inches and estimated his weight at two hundred pounds.

What was left of Corbet's face was smashed. I kneeled next to the body, then struggled to describe it in factual language. I noted suborbital lacerations, cut-like defects on the nose and lips, and a compound fracture of the right mandible – his broken jaw bone stuck through the skin. The damage was hard to document because of the blood on his face, neck, shirt and coat. Dead leaves, twigs, and glass pebbles mingled with his blood. I photographed them, then picked them up with tweezers and bagged them.

Corbet's topcoat was open, and I saw he was dressed for the office, not the extreme cold. He wore a starched blue dress shirt, blue striped tie, black leather belt with a gold metal buckle, and a navy suit. I cut a small hole in the dress shirt beneath his ribs, and took his body core temperature with a meat thermometer. I didn't use the professional forensic thermometers – they weren't as exact. I circled and initialed the cut I'd made in Corbet's pale skin and also in his shirt, so the ME would know I'd made the mark.

I could see the steering wheel imprint on his blood-drenched chest. I photographed that, too. Corbet's suit appeared clean and pressed but the knees were shiny. He wore no boots or waterproof shoe covers, only polished black lace-up dress shoes with salt stains along the edges. The shoes' new half-soles were encrusted with crushed road salt except where I saw the impression of the gas pedal on his right shoe sole.

I photographed the shoes, then said, "Detective, did you see this?" I pointed to the right sole. "Here's the evidence he crashed with his foot on the gas pedal."

The detective squatted to look, then shook his head. "Another sign of suicide."

"Did he leave a note?"

"Haven't found it yet."

"He may have been on hard times," I said. "He has a good watch, but the band needs to be replaced, his suit pants are shiny, and his shoes have been re-soled at least once."

"Maybe he's just cheap. Aren't rich people frugal?"

"The ones who don't go into an office are more likely to dress like bums. This man worked somewhere."

I stood up, brushing snow and dead leaves off my pants. "I'm finished." My teeth were chattering.

A plain black van parked next to the detective's unmarked car.

"Good timing," Jace said. "The morgue van is here."

I gave Jace points for that. Less sensitive cops called it the meat wagon. I made sure the body was properly tagged and the paperwork in order, then the attendants quickly loaded the body, slammed the doors, and tried to take off. The van, stuck in a snow drift, rocked and roared, then fish-tailed and broke free.

"I'll go with you to break the news to Mrs. Corbet," Jace said. "Helluva thing to have to tell a wife during the holidays."

I flashed back to the young uniform on my doorstep the day Donegan had his fatal heart attack and my heart twisted.

"Helluva thing to have to tell a wife any time." I was trembling, and not only from the bitter cold.

CHAPTER 6

Tuesday, December 27, 5:37 p.m.

Delano Corbet's three-story mansion looked impressive – from a distance. The Tiffany stained-glass windows glowed in the setting sun. Up close, I saw the drive wasn't plowed, the hedges needed pruning, and the trim could use a coat of paint.

Jace and I parked our cars in the circular drive. The detective rang the bell, and a fifty-something blonde in a beige cable-knit sweater answered the door.

"Mrs. Corbet?" Jace asked.

She might have been attractive, but I couldn't tell. Before we could introduce ourselves, she screamed, "No! He's dead! Del's dead. No! No! No!" She beat her head against the door jamb.

Jace and I gently stopped her, then half-carried the weeping woman into a pale green living room. I settled her in a tapestry wing chair, found a tissue for her, then introduced myself. "Mrs. Corbet, were you expecting this news?"

She blew her nose. "It's Iris. Iris Corbet."

I could see the remnants of a haunting beauty in Iris's tired, fine-boned face. Her faded blue eyes were red with worry and bruised with dark circles. Her makeup-free face was blotched and pale. She clutched the crumpled tissue and fought to control her tears. "I knew something was wrong ever since Del called me this morning."

"Was your husband at work this morning?" I asked.

Iris shook her head. "He lost his job ten months ago. My husband was a broker with Hanley and Hobart."

The most successful firm in the Forest. Even Jace knew that. "H&H was letting staff go?" he asked.

"Del didn't make his quota." Iris looked sad, then turned defiant. "That's what they said. But you want to know the real reason? He was old and tired. Del gave his life to that company. *His life!* Old Mr. Hobart appreciated that, but when he retired, the new management didn't care. They gave him some severance, but this house ate it up."

She opened her arms to take in the vast room, and I realized how empty it was – and how threadbare. I saw four large, pale rectangular spots on the grass-cloth wallpaper. Did the Corbets sell their art? The chandelier was Waterford crystal, but the room was missing the usual pricey, frivolous knickknacks. No candlesticks on the empty fireplace, no porcelain, silver, or cut glass. Had they been sold, too? The house wasn't decorated for the holidays, not even a wreath on the door, defying Forest custom.

"We can't sell this white elephant. Friends lent us some money, but that's gone, too. We're barely getting by."

Iris was shivering uncontrollably. The room was so cold I suspected the heat was off. I pulled a throw off the beige couch and realized it hid a hole in the fabric. I pretended not to notice, and wrapped the new widow in the warm blanket.

"How did Del die?" Iris asked.

Jace hesitated, and her anger flared up in the awkward silence. "Was it his car? His God damned money-eating car? He could have sold it for almost thirty thousand dollars and bought something reasonable, but no, he had to keep up appearances. He said to make money we had to look like we already had it."

I suspected Iris raged at the car to avoid blaming the man who'd abandoned her.

She repeated her question, minus the anger. "Please tell me how my husband died."

"His car went off the road," Jace said, "and hit a tree."

She flinched. "Did he suffer?"

I pushed away the vision of the tree branch spearing Corbet's eye.

"It was quick." Jace avoided the answer. "You were telling us your husband lost his job."

"Del's been looking for work. He called everyone he knew, cashed in every favor, reached out to every contact, but he couldn't find anything."

"Is that where he was going today?" Jace asked gently. "He looked like he was dressed for a job interview."

"Today ..." she said, and stopped. "Today ..." she tried again. "Today he thought he was going to finally get a job.

"Yesterday, Del got a callback from a company where he'd interviewed two weeks ago. The human resources manager asked him to come in at ten this morning. Del was sure he'd be hired."

She studied her hands and tried to talk again, but her words were drowned in tears. I handed her a box of tissues that had been sitting on a lamp table. Iris dried her eyes, blew her nose, then took a deep breath and spoke quickly, as if she was afraid she'd lose her words in another tear storm:

"This morning, Del woke up cheerful, ate a big breakfast, and whistled while he dressed. He –" she stopped, then plunged ahead as if she was diving into icy water. "He kissed me goodbye and said we'd go out and celebrate tonight."

The silence stretched on. Somewhere, I heard a clock ticking.

"He didn't get the job?" Jace prompted.

Now Iris's voice was thick with tears – and anger. "The idiot at human resources said she wanted to give Del the 'courtesy' of telling him in person! Del called me afterward. He was crying. Del never cries. Never! He said he couldn't face coming home. He said he loved me."

Her voice broke. "I said, 'If you love me, you'll come home now.'

"He said ... he said, 'The life insurance will take care of you' and the phone went dead. All day long, I've called and texted him. I called everyone I know, asking if they've seen him."

More confirmation this was suicide. I said, "May I ask you a few questions, please?"

Iris nodded. I opened the Possible Self-Inflicted Injury form on my iPad. I knew the questions by heart, and Iris had already answered most of them. Yes, Del Corbet was depressed. No, he didn't leave a note, but he'd told his wife goodbye. I had only a few more questions:

"How long was your husband depressed?"

"I saw the first signs about six months ago. He'd been out of work four months by then, and it was wearing him down."

"Was your husband under a doctor's care?"

"He saw Doc Bartlett. She was his internist."

"Was he seeing anyone for depression?"

"No, he was afraid. The Forest is a small town. Del said it would hurt his job prospects if word got out he was going to a counselor."

"Did he take any medication?"

"Something for high cholesterol. That's all."

"Did he ever talk about suicide?"

"Not really. He was worried. We both are. But I thought we'd get through this. He did say his life insurance didn't have a suicide clause."

"What's that mean?"

"If he killed himself, I'd still collect a million dollars. I don't want the damn money." Iris started weeping again.

I waited until the new widow dried her eyes. "When did your husband mention the suicide clause?"

"About six weeks ago."

"Did Mr. Corbet drink?"

"He's a social drinker." Iris sniffed. More tears welled up, and I handed her another tissue. "He likes scotch. Single malt." Iris smiled sadly and nodded toward the nearly empty pricey liquor bottles lined up on the polished sideboard. "We haven't been able to afford good liquor for some time."

Until today. Instead of coming home to celebrate his new job with his wife, Delano Corbet bought a fifth of courage, slammed into a tree, and made her a millionaire.

"Do you have someone who can stay with you?"

"My sister, Melanie."

"Would you like me to call her?"

"I'll call. Will you stay here until she shows up?"

Fifteen minutes later, Melanie, an older, grayer version of Iris, arrived. Jace and I left the sisters to a tearful reunion.

Outside, the cold was like a stinging slap. "That poor woman." Jace shook his head.

I didn't want to rehash the awful scene. "Any word on the search for Juliet?"

The detective checked his cell phone. "Nothing. I'm worried she's dead, Angela. The temperature has stayed below zero all day. I tried to trace her movements. The last time anyone saw her was when she left the party at Bella Du Pres's house, just before midnight. That's about all I can find out, except there was a lot of drinking. Bella's parents wouldn't let her talk to me."

"That's outrageous."

Jace shrugged. "I gather that's what people are like here. They law-yer-up at the first excuse."

"But Juliet's one of their own. I thought sure they'd talk to you. I have some news." I told the detective about Juliet's forbidden Toonerville boyfriend, Dexter Gordon.

"It's a start. Are you going to the ME's office next?"

"Yeah, I want to file this DI report."

"I have to stop there and talk to a security guard about another case. Want to get some coffee in the cafeteria?"

I knew he wasn't coming onto me. Jace was happily married with a son. "I'm really tired. I'd like to go home. But avoid the hospital coffee. I'd rather drink the cafeteria's dishwater. Get the stuff out of the machine, Detective. Trust me, it's better."

I waved good-bye and drove off. The medical examiner's office was at the back of Sisters of Sorrow Hospital, and the hunt for Juliet had extended to the parking lot. I saw the searchers going from car to car in the vast SOS parking lot.

I didn't really have an office. The ME took most of my allotted cubicle space for a shower in his oversized executive suite. I got a narrow desk and a decade-old computer terminal, with a bonus – my freedom. During my shift, I didn't have to stick around the office, as long as I could be quickly reached.

I struggled with Delano Corbet's death investigation report. I couldn't get the gruesome vision of the dead man out of my mind, or Iris's grief. His widow had lost her husband and her peace of mind. She would forever wonder if she could have saved him.

Corbet's suicide led to another awful thought: What if Juliet had killed herself? My stomach clenched. She'd had a fight with Brock, a Forest blue blood who'd wanted to have sex with her. Brock called her a slut and slammed his fist into a wall. Bella told Juliet that her first lover, Dex, had laughed at her body and her romantic notions, and insulted her sexuality. Bella's mother made her cry, then gave Juliet a mysterious white powder. Juliet was drunk on beer and vodka when she left with Dex. Teenage girls could be emotional and unstable. Did Juliet kill herself after that horrible evening?

I was sick at the possibility. I finished my report, then hurried to the office of my friend, Dr. Katie Kelly Stern, the assistant Chouteau County ME.

Brown-haired Katie, practical as a pair of wool gloves, should have been plain, but her sense of humor and quick wit added charm to her ordinary looks. She had captivated the Forest's most eligible lawyer, Montgomery Bryant.

Katie was typing at her desk in her closet-sized office. When she saw me in her doorway, Katie looked alarmed. "Angela! What's wrong? You look like a week's worth of bad news."

"Nothing serious. Just a bad death investigation."

"The guy who slammed into the tree? I saw what was left of him."

"That's him. Delano Corbet. His wife is devastated." I told Katie the story. "Iris said he called and told her he couldn't face coming home, but he loved her. He must have hung up, then drank scotch and drove around until he got the nerve to crash into the tree."

"That was thoughtless," Katie said. "And cruel."

"I think he was in so much pain he didn't realize the effect his death would have on Iris." I squeezed into Katie's guest chair and bumped my knees on the desk.

Katie studied my face. "It's also affected another widow, Angela Richman. That's why you look like recycled shit."

I hurried to change the subject, and tell her my fear. "Suicide death investigations are always bad. I'm worried we have another one." I told Katie how I'd been pulled into the search for Juliet and my encounters with the missing girl's two friends. "I don't like either one."

Katie shrugged. "That's what kids are like. I'd be tempted to slap Daisy. Bella just needs to be locked in a closet and not allowed out until she's at least thirty. Honesty, my ass. The mean girl mentality is alive and kicking."

"Last time I checked, you didn't have any kids, Katie. When did you get to be an expert on teenagers?"

"When I was growing up, my fifteen-year-old cousin lived with us for two years. Two long years." Katie tried to lean back in her chair, but there wasn't room. She'd papered the wall behind her desk with an autumn woods scene. Lurking between the tree trunks was a plastic skull glued to the wall. It was wearing a plastic poinsettia – the only sign of the holidays in her room.

"You haven't taken down your Christmas decorations yet," I said.

Katie looked up and smiled. "Tradition says you keep them up until after the twelve days of Christmas. It's more like the twelve years of Christmas now that Monty's sixteen-year-old nephew Nate is staying with him for the holidays. He's here to give Monty's sister in California a break. The kid's been running wild since his father took off with his secretary."

"Couldn't Dad have a more original mid-life crisis?" I crossed my legs and whacked my shin on the desk.

"I know, it's a cliche. That's why it happens. Nate's mad at his dad and lashing out. He wants to be a lawyer with the Innocence Project, but he's also a car nut. Seems to me he's been talking about a kid named Dex, who works on hot cars."

"Really? Was Nate at the party last night?"

Katie rolled her eyes. "How long have you lived in the Forest? Dex is a Toonerville kid. I have no idea how he wheedled an invite to Bella's party, but I know damn well Dex doesn't have the clout to invite his friends."

I suddenly felt a small surge of hope. "Could I talk to Nate about Dex?"

"Hell, you can have him for the rest of the holiday. I haven't had more than half an hour alone with Monty since the kid got here. I can't wait to pack him back on the plane New Year's Day. Then it will truly be a happy New Year."

"When can I talk to him?"

"He's with Monty at the law office. I'll text him right now." The exchange was quickly completed. Katie's cell phone pinged, and she told me, "You're all set. You can come over."

"Can I bring anything?"

"Maybe a pizza. Make that two pizzas. Nate can eat a whole one by himself."

I started to stand up. "Wait! I got off the track when we were talking about mean girls. Do you think Juliet could have committed suicide?"

After I laid out why I was worried, especially Juliet's boy trouble, Katie said, "Good lord! How did this girl get lost with every boy in the Forest chasing after her?"

"Maybe that was part of the problem."

"Did Juliet make any statements that sounded suicidal?"

"She told Bella that Dex was the only boy she ever loved and if he didn't love her, she'd kill herself. Daisy claims Juliet never said anything about killing herself."

"Still, that doesn't sound good." Katie steepled her fingers.

"She definitely left the party with Dex and she hasn't been seen since," I said.

Katie's chair creaked. "Juliet's under a lot of pressure at her age. That's tough. We had another suicide here in November – a sixteen-year-old Toonerville girl who broke up with her boyfriend. That's one big reason why kids kill themselves. At that age they can't think past next week. With their hormones raging, they take everything too hard."

I felt sick. "How would she kill herself?"

"*If* she killed herself. Girls tend to be cutters or take pills. A romantic like Juliet would probably take pills. That's what the Toonerville girl did. Girls think they'll die romantically and look beautiful. They don't realize they'll be puking their guts out and shitting themselves."

"Where would Juliet get the pills?"

"From her friends, though her group seems pretty straight. Daisy's brother Rick said that, right?"

"He said Daisy didn't use pot."

"And they hang out at the Olive Garden, not the mini mart? That's where kids would be exchanging pills – often ones they stole from their parents' prescriptions."

"Maybe I should ask Juliet's mother if she's missing any pain pills."

Katie sat straight up. "Whoa! Maybe you should think about avoiding career suicide. You can't call up Midge LaRouche and say, 'Wanna check your oxy supply? Could be your darling daughter's offed herself with mother's little helpers.'"

"If it would save Juliet's life, I would."

"Very noble. Also, freaking useless. Who's running this case now that Greiman and Chetkin are out?"

"The new detective, Jace Budewitz."

"He's a cutie, and he's got that all-American look. Let him ask the tough questions. Where's he at?"

"I think he's still here. He had to talk to a guard, then he wanted to warm up with some coffee in the SOS cafeteria."

"Go track him down. Get him to pop the hard questions. That's his job. Then go pick up those pizzas and talk to Nate and Monty."

I found the detective sitting at a table in the cafeteria, reading a newspaper and drinking machine coffee. He smiled at me. "Are you sure this is better than the cafeteria coffee, Angela? It tastes like chicken soup. The machine dispenses that, too."

"Trust me, even soup-flavored coffee beats the hospital brew." I sat down across from him. "Listen, do you think Juliet may have committed suicide?"

Jace looked surprised. "Never occurred to me. I'm more used to street kids. These rich kids' problems don't seem real."

"They're very real. They're under tremendous pressure from their families. Last year, a Forest girl nearly killed herself because she didn't get into the Ivy League school her parents wanted. She barely survived."

Jace shook his head. "That's terrible. I don't know how these people think. They're so different from the street types."

"Look close and they're surprisingly alike. They're gangs in designer labels, motivated by greed and fear of work."

"Well, when you put it that way ..." Jace smiled. "If she tried to kill herself, it's good we're dealing with a girl."

"Katie said girls either cut themselves or use pills."

"Right. They're easier to save than boys, who use guns or hang themselves. Often the girls don't take enough pills, so we can pump their stomachs. I'll ask Juliet's mother if she's missing any prescription meds."

Good, I thought. He took the bait.

Jace stood up, and tossed the paper and half-empty coffee cup in the trash. "We'd better find Juliet soon. Whether she's lost or she's suicidal, her chances are running out."

CHAPTER 7

Tuesday, December 27, 7:37 p.m.

Before I drove to Monty's law office, I checked the local TV station on my iPad, hoping I'd hear good news. Instead, I saw a clip of Midge LaRouche pleading for her daughter's life again.

"Please." Midge's voice was hoarse with tears. "If you saw Juliet any time after midnight Monday – that's actually today, Tuesday – please call me. Or call the tip line, if you want to be anonymous. No questions asked. *Any* tiny bit of information can lead to Juliet's safe return. No matter how unimportant it sounds, *please* call.

"And Juliet, honey, if you're staying overnight with a friend, please call your daddy or me. You won't be in trouble, we promise. We just want to make sure you're safe." The sentence seemed to be cut off in mid-sob.

Midge's heartrending pleas were underscored by the solemn announcer and a grim video of hopeless searchers on a gray day: "Hundreds of searchers have been looking for Juliet LaRouche in Chouteau County, but so far there is no trace of the missing sixteen-year-old. Juliet's parents have offered a reward of $25,000 for the safe return of their daughter, a Chouteau Forest Academy honor student."

Not good, I thought. Not good at all. The sickly winter daylight had faded, along with Juliet's chances for survival. I prayed the girl was safe and warm with her boyfriend or sulking at a friend's house.

Overhead, I heard the *whump, whump* of a helicopter – Juliet's search had expanded to the air. Monty's law office was near SOS. Other, less successful lawyers said the location made it easier for him to chase ambulances. I had to swing through Toonerville to pick up the two pepperoni pizzas. Now they perfumed my car, but I'd lost my appetite. As I drove through Toonerville, groups of bundled searchers combed the small yards, checking tool sheds and looking in garages for the missing girl.

At Monty's office, the lights were warm and welcoming. I parked in the circular drive, and the lawyer opened the double brass doors and hurried out to meet me with a hearty welcome. "Angela! You brought pizza. Come in, come in. You'll freeze."

To call Montgomery Bryant handsome was like saying the weather was cold. The man was breathtaking—broad shoulders, thick brown hair, eyes the color of new blue jeans. Better yet, he didn't seem to realize his startling good looks.

Young Nate had the early signs of his uncle's good looks – the same dark hair and dark blue eyes with long, smoky eyelashes. Now the kid was a scrawny six feet tall and couldn't figure out what to do with his hands and feet. Monty handed him the pizza boxes.

"Angela, meet my nephew, Nate Bryant."

Nate turned dark red with embarrassment and managed a hello. "Nate's the strong, silent type," Monty said. "He wants to be a pro bono lawyer."

The boy nodded, tripped over nothing, and shambled into the law office's staff room where napkins, soft drinks and paper plates were waiting on a round table. The two men dug into the pizzas. I picked at a slice on a plate.

"Any word on the missing girl?" Monty asked.

I shook my head. "It seems like the whole Forest is searching for Juliet, but so far, nothing. The temperature's dropping, Monty. If Juliet's outside, she doesn't have a chance."

Nate looked stricken, though I wasn't sure why. "I think Nate knows Dex, her boyfriend," Monty said.

Nate had just taken a gigantic bite of pizza. He nodded and turned a deeper shade of red. We watched him chew, which seemed to embarrass Nate even more. I felt sorry for the kid and tried to start a conversation. "I understand Dex restores old cars."

Nate finally swallowed the pizza, Adam's apple bobbing. He took a drink of Mountain Dew. "Yeah, I got to ride in his GOAT." I knew that was the nickname for a GTO.

"Now he's working on another amazing old car. A '79 Camaro with headers, and a scoop through the hood. The hot cars are different here than in California. Here there aren't many JDMs."

"What's that? I thought I knew my cars."

"A Japanese domestic market car," he said. "Mostly Honda Civics and Nissan 240 SXes. You can get them cheap – under four thousand. In California, they like them super low and sleek. The other thing they look for is old Beemers. The older and smaller the better."

"I've seen a few Subaru WRXs out and about," I said. "Some have been worked on, but most of it's under the hood. The Forest kids go for Jeeps or Mustangs, and those tend to get ordered from the factory with the performance kits."

"Mustangs?" Nate rolled his eyes. "That's a dad car."

I cut off the car talk. "Nate, I need your opinion. Dex was the last person seen with Juliet. Do you think he'd hurt her?"

Nate seemed flattered he'd been asked a serious question. He chewed thoughtfully, then said, "No. I haven't known him long, just a few days. But Dex is a cool guy who really likes Juliet. Now it's all turned to shit, and he doesn't know how to fix it."

"How did it go wrong?" I asked.

"He got drunk at the party at Bella's house. She's part of Juliet's crowd. Dex isn't."

"They look down on him because his dad's a mechanic," I said.

Nate gulped another hunk of pizza, then nodded. "I think it's cool Dex can fix cars, but in Juliet's crowd it's who you know and who your parents are. Dex knew he didn't belong at that party. He was only there because Juliet wanted him to come. She left him alone to talk to her girlfriends and he heard some dudes laughing at him and calling him a greaser."

"How do you know this?" I asked.

"Dex texted me about the party this morning." Nate's next bite was a third of a slice, and we waited for him to finish chewing.

"Dex told me he didn't care what those dick– uh, dudes – said about him, but I think he did. That's probably why he said some stuff he shouldn't have, and Juliet got in his face about it. Dex told her she shouldn't take it seriously."

Typical male response, I thought, but stuffed my mouth with pizza so I wouldn't interrupt this sudden flow of information.

"Juliet started crying and said she wanted to go home because he'd humiliated her. Dex didn't know what to do. When girls cry, it's like weird."

"She had good reasons to cry," I said. "Her friends told me Dex had laughed at Juliet's –" I stopped, suddenly embarrassed. Nate turned flame red. "Her small breasts," I said. "She's a very romantic young woman and he made fun of her."

Now I wondered if Dex's carelessly cruel words had mortally wounded the girl. Nate was probably the only person who knew what happened to Juliet after the party. I glanced at Monty. He nodded slightly, then casually snagged another piece of pizza.

"What happened on the ride home from Bella's?" I hoped my question sounded natural.

"Dex was driving super slow because he was hammered and he

didn't want to get stopped by the cops. They don't bother the rich kids, but Dex is from – what's the name they use for his part of town?"

"Toonerville," I said.

"Right. Stupid name. Why's it called that?"

"It's from an old-time comic strip about a rickety trolley," Monty said. "It means some place rundown. You were telling us Dex was drunk when he left the party."

"Dex was like totally tanked, and he tried to explain to Juliet, but he made it worse instead."

I thought about what Bella had told me, about Dex laughing with the boys saying: *Juliet thought this was true love, when all he wanted was a fuck. He said rich girls didn't screw as well as poor ones. He laughed about her small tits.* How did a sixteen-year-old boy excuse those words?

"What did he say?" Monty asked.

"She was crying and then she said she'd given him her … uh … virginity." Nate turned stoplight red at that word.

Uh-oh, I thought.

"Dex tried to make her feel better. He said popping your cherry shouldn't be a big deal – it wasn't for him – and then she really got upset."

I kept quiet. So did Monty. Nate filled the silence. "Dex was almost at her house by then and Juliet screamed that he had to let her out of the car *right now*. He said Juliet would freeze – she wasn't wearing a decent coat or anything. 'If you don't stop the car, I'll jump and maybe break a leg or die,' she told him, 'and it will be all your fault.'"

"Dex texted you all that?" I asked.

Nate looked uneasy and turned red again. This time, I thought guilt, not teenage awkwardness, had tied his tongue.

"What did you do, Nate?" Monty asked.

"Uh."

"I won't send you home early, but I have to know," he said.

Now the words rushed out. "He texted me about two-fifteen or so this morning. Dex was really scared and wanted to meet up, but I said I didn't have a car. He said he'd pick me up on the street by your house. I had to help him. He's my friend."

"So you got in the car with a drunken driver," Monty said.

Nate hung his head.

"Then what?" Monty asked.

"On the way to his house, Dex told me what happened. He'd wanted to drive Juliet all the way to her house, but she was afraid Mrs. Ellis – the housekeeper – would hear his car.

"She jumped out when Dex slowed down at the stop sign. Dex never saw her again."

"That's a killing cold," Monty said. "What happened next? That girl's life is at stake."

"Nothing. He was afraid to go back for her. She was too pissed. He drove home and texted me, and then he picked me up.

"When we got to Dex's house, his parents were asleep, so we sneaked into his room. I could hear them snoring when we were in the hallway. Dex said they were probably drunk. He stuffed a rug under his bedroom door and then we talked."

"Did he try to reach that girl?" Monty asked.

"Yes! Lots of times. He kept texting Juliet. He even called her, but she wouldn't answer. Juliet does that sometimes when she's mad, he said. Then he got a call from Mrs. Ellis. She was scary mad, demanding to know where Juliet was. She'd called Bella – that's the girl who gave the party – and woke her up and Bella told the old lady that Juliet and Dex had left about twenty till midnight. Juliet should have been home by midnight, and it was one-thirty in the morning.

"Mrs. Ellis had flipped out and demanded Dex's cell phone number, and Bella gave it up. She doesn't like him."

"Wait," Monty said. "How does Bella know Dex's cell number if she doesn't like him?"

"Juliet's crowd used Dex to help bypass the camera system at some rich kid's house. They hang out there when the family's out of town."

"The Minterns," I said. "I went there today with Daisy, looking for Juliet. She wasn't there."

"After the housekeeper got Dex's number, she called him," Monty prompted.

"Yes," Nate said. "Dex was still too jagged up to answer his phone. The housekeeper went apeshit and called Juliet's parents in Colorado."

"And the LaRouches flew home on their private plane," I said.

Nate nodded. "They were home by five that morning. Soon as the plane touched down, Juliet's dad called Dex's cell. Dex was afraid to answer. Old Man LaRouche left a message reaming him. He said if Dex didn't pick up he'd call Bella again to get Dex's address.

"I don't know why he had to call Bella for the address. He could have just looked it up online. But Dex knew he was in deep shit. Old Man LaRouche is so rich he can crush Dex's family.

"I said he'd have to bite the bullet and tell his parents. He said his dad would beat the crap out of him, but we didn't see any other way out of it. Dex told me to go hide in the basement, and if things got bad, I should sneak out the basement door.

"So I did. The stairs were creaky and the basement was a mess – old broken junk, dusty boxes, piles of dirty laundry. It stank, too. I used my cell phone flashlight to see and still hit my shin on something. It hurt really bad."

Nate stopped, possibly hoping for sympathy. Monty glared at the kid. "Go on." Nate gulped and continued.

"I could hear Dex's dad screaming at him and throwing stuff. Lots of thuds and a crash, like a broken glass or bottle. His mom was trying to calm his father down."

"He was assaulting his son and you didn't call me or the police?" Monty's face was dark with anger.

"I couldn't," Nate said. "There wasn't time. I heard a car or an SUV

– something big – screech into the driveway. I looked out the basement window and saw Old Man LaRouche. He was insane. Pounding on the door, yelling, shouting threats. I bet he woke up the whole the street.

"Dex's father wouldn't let LaRouche inside. He was still yelling at Dex. I could hear Dex's mother crying."

"She did nothing to help her son?" I asked.

"She never does," Nate said. "Dex says she's afraid of her husband. The basement door opened, and he practically threw Dex down the stairs. Dex landed at the bottom in some dirty laundry. I think it broke his fall. Dex was shaking, he was so upset, but LaRouche got there before Dex's father could really hurt him.

"We heard Juliet's dad barge in and stomp around, screaming he was going to throw them all in jail. Then he took off. It was quiet for a little while, except for Dex's mom crying. His parents talked too softly for us to hear anything, and then we heard drawers being opened and doors slammed. Next the basement door opened, and a duffle bag came flying down the stairs.

"'Those are your clothes, dipshit,' his father said. 'The keys to the shop's loaner car are in the side pocket. You're going to drive to your grandparents' house in St. Louis and stay there until this blows over. Now get out! You sicken me.'

"Dex took the duffle bag and motioned me to follow him. We went out the basement door and got into this silver Toyota. It's like the invisible car. Dex apologized for all the trouble and dropped me off at your place. You were still asleep."

"And you didn't wake me to tell me your friend had been beaten by his father and was on the run?" Monty said.

Nate said nothing.

"Is Dex in St. Louis now?" Monty asked.

"No. He didn't want to stay with the wrinklies. His grandparents don't have Wi-Fi, and they're almost as mean as his dad. He said he'd get in touch with me later. I haven't heard from him since nine this morning."

Nate crammed another pizza slice in his mouth as if he hadn't eaten for a week.

I broke the tense silence. "Juliet's parents didn't tell me any of this when I talked with them. Detective Budewitz, who's in charge of the investigation, doesn't know it. Bella's parents wouldn't let her talk to him. I don't get it. What are the LaRouches hiding, Monty? Why didn't they mention Dex?"

Monty looked disgusted. "I'm guessing Midge doesn't want the Forest to know her precious daughter's dating a low-rent mechanic's son from Toonerville."

"She was doing more than dating him," Nate said, and Monty glared him into silence.

"And they'll risk their daughter's life to keep that from the police?" I asked.

"Midge is concerned about Juliet's future. Even I know they have big plans for that girl. Juliet's on track to be a Daughter of Versailles Queen."

I couldn't control my rage. "She'll be queen of the dead instead. Her parents are holding back vital information but crying about her to the media. Jace Budewitz needs to know this. Right now. I'll tell him." I pulled out my cell phone.

"Angela, calm down. Nate will talk to the detective. He's my nephew and we'll do this together." The boy looked wide-eyed and scared.

Monty stood up and hugged me. That was my cue to leave. "Thanks for bringing us dinner, Angela," he said. "You look beat. Please go home. You've had a long day. I'll text you any new developments."

I was shivering with rage as I drove home. Damn the LaRouches. And Bella Du Pres's family. Snobs! Cowards!

I saw more searchers, their flashlights like fireflies in the dark, their cries of "Juliet!" echoing with sad futility in the frigid air.

CHAPTER 8

Tuesday, December 27, 8:12 p.m.

My home was freezing. The former guest house was impossible to insulate. The white stone walls held in the cold and the winter wind whistled through the windows. I upped the thermostat to nearly eighty, put on my shaggy brown robe that made me look like a hibernating bear, and fixed myself hot chocolate.

I tried to settle in on the living room couch and watch TV. The show was interrupted twice with local Juliet updates. The hair-sprayed blonde looked coolly at the camera. "The search continues for missing Juliet LaRouche, but there are no new leads in the disappearance of the sixteen-year-old Chouteau Forest Academy student."

This time, when I saw a teary-eyed Midge weeping and begging, "Please give me *any* information about my daughter, anything at all," I wanted to throw my chocolate mug at the TV. I shouted at the screen, "Then why didn't you tell the police she left the party with Dexter?"

A news feature on hypothermia interrupted my pointless commentary, ending with handy information on what happens when a person's core temperature drops below 95 degrees. The reporter declared:

"The signs of hypothermia include uncontrollable shivering, mumbling, stumbling, gray or blue-tinged skin, drowsiness and shallow breathing."

I was back talking to the TV. "Are you watching, Midge and Prentice? Your beautiful daughter could be a snow queen instead of a DV Queen. Because you won't tell the police what happened."

My useless rant was interrupted by a cell phone chime. Monty texted me, *Dex's parents confirm the boy never reached his grandparents' house. Police are searching for him.*

For the first time, I felt a slight bloom of hope. Now the search would make progress. I tried watching *Forensic Files* and wondered why so many of the TV show's homicide cops had mustaches. A story about a lawyer murdered by his son was interrupted by a second text from Monty, *Dex's car was found at the West Forest Mall with a cell phone inside. Police say it's Juliet's. Search is on for both kids.*

I flicked through the stations. The missing teens' photos were shown on everyone, but the tone had changed. Now the stories were hard-edged, tense and excited. The announcers implied that Juliet had been murdered in a lover's quarrel, and Dexter was on the run. The TV news stories now showed Dex's photo and information. "The missing girl was last seen in the company of this sixteen-year-old boy, and their whereabouts are unknown," the blonde announcer said. In less than an hour, the search story had changed to a manhunt for a teen killer.

Juliet's parents seemed to be the only Forest dwellers clinging to the hope that Juliet would be found alive. On yet another TV interview, Midge looked thirty years older than the woman I'd talked to this morning. Her shoulders slumped, and her face sagged. Prentice stood at her side, stripped of his confidence, his eyes bleak. Midge could hardly force out the familiar plea. "Please. If you know anything ..." Then Midge dissolved into tears and Prentice held her.

I couldn't stand their pain – or their lies. I flicked off the TV. On the internet, I was bombarded with photos of Dex and Juliet. On Facebook, I saw the "Have you seen this teenager?" photos had more than 789 shares.

The comments in an online news story reflected the Forest's fears. "That innocent child was killed by Toonerville scum," **4estLadie** said. "Remember this, liberals, next time you want to end the death penalty," wrote **Gr8US**. **GodluvsMartha** wrote, "If Juliet has faith, the Lord is her protection." I wondered about the armies of innocents whose deaths I'd investigated: old people, children, even babies. Did God take the day off for them?

I didn't want to wrestle with theological thoughts. I called Katie and told her, "Monty's house guest has stirred up a real hornet's nest."

"Monty's been keeping me updated," Katie said. "It's the most we've talked since the kid got here. Actually, we still haven't talked. He's texted. He can't believe the kid sneaked out of the house last night to be with Dexter."

"Do you think she's still alive?"

"No way."

"So Dex killed her?"

"Can't tell. I don't know the boy, but Toonerville kids are easy to blame. Wanna come over? I've been living like a nun since Monty's nephew got here. Let's work on a bottle of Shiraz."

"Can't drink," I said. "Doesn't mix with my meds. But Shiraz goes well with chocolate. I'll stop for some."

"The Chocolate Shoppe at the West Forest Mall is having a clearance sale. I like dark chocolate with anything – except ants and crickets."

"You ate chocolate-covered bugs?"

"Hell, no. Some idiot thought because I encounter gruesome things in my job, I'd enjoy 'alternative' protein. I don't eat anything that can be killed with a can of Raid. See you soon."

My fatigue and depression had vanished. I shrugged out of my bear robe, threw on my warmest clothes, booted up, and ten minutes later was on my way to the mall. The night was clear, and the cold needle-sharp. I could see searchers were still combing the Forest fields by flashlight, their mournful cries of "Juliet!" rippling over the frozen ground.

At the mall, the shoppers were a sullen, dispirited bunch, drained of courtesy and Christmas cheer. A bald man nearly knocked me down as he pushed his way onto the escalator. I was tempted to whack him with my purse. I threaded though the food court, past counters selling Chinese food, pretzels, pizza, and the inevitable smoothies. Diners seemed to think that standing next to the smoothies' fresh fruit display while they waited for their greasy grub was a healthy choice. I was amazed how much food was tossed in the trash. Juliet's haunting photo was plastered on every pillar.

I found the Chocolate Shoppe by scent. The rich perfume of chocolate overpowered the food court's grease fog. I was greeted by a rosy-cheeked woman in a blue dirndl, who kept offering samples. I ate them all – chocolate turtles, chili-infused chocolate caramels, salted chocolate caramels, and four kinds of truffles. I liked – and bought – everything, and felt slightly queasy by the time the saleswoman packed my purchases into a slick brown shopping bag.

As I hurried toward the escalator, I heard a commotion in the food court. I saw a dark-haired teen boy rummaging in a trash can, holding a red plastic plate of what looked like fried rice.

"Hey, you! Stop!" shouted a thirty-something man in a blue parka. "You killed that girl."

The boy froze over the trash can like a raccoon caught scrounging in the garbage. "No!"

He was lying. I recognized him immediately. Dex was even better looking than his photos. He had a surly bad-boy charm and a face that was almost pretty. Thick, blue-black hair framed high cheekbones and blue eyes fringed with long lashes. He had big shoulders and smooth muscles.

Blue Parka moved closer to Dex, prepared for battle. Diners and shoppers whipped out their cell phones to record the drama as Dex dropped the fried rice and sprinted for the escalator. Blue Parka tackled the boy, and Dex hit the sharp escalator steps face first. Someone screamed. As Dex crawled away from the escalator, a second diner kicked him in the gut. The boy raised his arms to protect himself and a woman slammed him with an orange plastic chair.

"Stop!" I screamed. "Stop. You're killing him."

The crowd ignored me and kept kicking and beating the boy. I looked around wildly for help, then speed-dialed Detective Budewitz. He answered on the first ring.

"Help! We've got an emergency at the West Forest Mall. Dex was spotted in the food court and vigilantes are pounding the kid to pieces. He needs an ambulance. Bring reinforcements. It's a riot!"

"Call security. I'm on my way."

"Hurry, before you've got a homicide on your hands."

Where was security? Shoppers were whacking Dex with food trays, shopping bags, and suitcase-sized purses. A boy about five threw his orange soda in Dex's bloody face. A twenty-something woman kicked his shins.

I saw a tubby, sixtyish mall cop in a wrinkled beige uniform cruise over in a Segway. He parked and watched a woman lift a clay pot bursting with poinsettias from a holiday display and charge toward the battered teen.

"Stop her, officer!" I shouted. I spotted his name tag – MARTY. "Marty! Don't let her hit him."

"It's not my job to save killers," he said with a snarl.

I held up my cell phone and tried to sound as official as possible while I videoed the attack. "Officer Marty, my name is Angela Richman. I'm videoing you standing by while a young man is being beaten on mall property. This man appears to be Dexter Gordon. I've called a Forest police detective and he's on his way. Mr. Gordon has not been convicted of any crime. He is wanted by the police for questioning. He has already sustained significant damage. I can see that his face is bleeding" – I zoomed in on the boy's head – "and he has cuts and bruises on his arms and legs." I panned his body, then stopped at his left arm, now hanging limply at his side. "His arm appears to be either sprained or broken. His coat and scarf are torn. So far, you have done nothing to stop this attack. If Dexter sues this mall for damages, I'll testify that you did not stop the attack."

Now Marty the mall cop waded into the crowd, shouting in a deep voice: "Time to leave, people. The police are on the way. You, sir! Put that chair down immediately."

The older man wielding the chair said, "Goddamn killer! You're gonna let him go free."

"No, sir. I'm going to detain him so the police can arrest him. If you don't set down that chair, you'll be arrested, too." The man put the chair back at a table and disappeared.

"Put down that flower pot, ma'am," Marty said to the woman about to crown Dex with poinsettias. "If you break it, you'll pay for it."

The Christmas flowers were returned to the display. The shoppers were melting away, picking up shopping bags and gathering children. Some stayed in small, gossiping groups, but no one attacked Dex. Marty helped the battered boy to an empty chair at a table piled with food trays, and brought a wad of napkins. Dex held them to his bloody face. I was horrified to see how quickly they were soaked with blood. His left arm lay in his lap.

"Dex," I said. "Help is on the way. Where are you hurt? Can you talk?"

"I didn't kill her," he said. "I love her."

"Then help us find Juliet."

He tried to raise his left arm and cried out in pain.

"The paramedics will be here shortly," I said, brushing his bloody hair out of his eyes. I was relieved to see Jace running through the exit doors, flanked by at least six uniforms. I waved to him. The last of the crowd vanished when they saw the police.

Marty the mall cop stepped forward, puffing out his chest. "I have the situation under control, Detective. Unfortunately, the suspect has sustained some damage."

"Some damage?" Jace roared. "He's had the crap beaten out of him. He'll be photographed before we leave, and I'll file a report with the mall that he didn't get these injuries in our custody. Now, Marty, you're going to help my officers find the vigilantes who beat this boy and then you're going to turn over the security tapes to my officers so we can track down the others. Got that?"

The mall cop nodded.

Jace turned to Dex. "How are you, Dexter?"

The boy looked white and shocky. "I think my arm's broken. My head hurts and my face won't stop bleeding. It hurts to breathe. I got kicked in the ribs."

"Help is on the way. I'll call your parents."

Dexter turned flour white under the red blood and the words rushed out. "No! My dad will beat me worse. He wouldn't let me talk to Mr. LaRouche. He said because I was from Toonerville they'd blame me and I'd go to jail. He told me to go to Gran and Grandpa's house until this died down, but I thought I could hide out at the mall."

Dex hung his bloody, bruised head. "Just go ahead and read me my rights and arrest me. I'm starving."

"I'm not going to arrest you yet. You are not in custody. You're going to the hospital as soon as the paramedics get here. We are actively searching for the people who beat you."

Dex looked surprised. "You're not going to arrest me?"

Jace dodged the question. "I need you to tell me everything that happened the last time you saw Juliet."

"I love Juliet. We had a stupid fight and she jumped out of my car at the stop sign by her house. We'd been at the party and I was drunk.

I tried to get her to stop drinking. I was mixing all sorts of shit – beer and vodka. She was, too. I had to get her out of there. I was taking her home for her own good. When we got close to her house she wanted to get out right then and go home through the woods. She opened the car door when I slowed down at the stop sign and nearly fell on her a– nearly fell down. She ran into the woods and screamed at me not to follow her. She was so mad at me."

"Why was she angry?" Jace asked.

"Because I'd been talking to another girl at the party."

I knew the boy was lying.

"I keep trying to text and call her to apologize, but she won't answer."

The police found Juliet's cell phone in his car, I thought. What's going on here?

"I had no idea Juliet was missing until her dad came to my house screaming like a crazy man. That's when my parents made me hide and then said I'd have to go to my grandparents in St. Louis."

Jace tried to stop the rush of words. "Whoa, whoa, okay, I get it. Now, before the paramedics take you to the hospital, do you feel well enough to show us the spot where Juliet exited your car?"

"Yeah, sure, that's what I wanted to do all along. My head hurts, but I'll do it."

"Okay, here come the paramedics. They'll load you up and drive by her house. You can show us where you left her off."

"That's all I want. My head hurts bad. Can they give me something for it?"

Dex was ghost white now. The blood on his face looked almost black in the sickly artificial light. He toppled face forward on the dirty table.

Dex was unconscious.

CHAPTER 9

Wednesday, December 28, 9:12 a.m.

The helicopters' *whap! whap! whap!* woke me up the next morning. I had a chocolate hangover, a grainy, headachy feeling after I'd pigged out last night at Katie's.

I dragged myself out of bed. Outside my window, the search for Juliet continued. I saw an awkward army of searchers, bundled in heavy clothes, moving slowly across the Du Pres property. A knot of people were looking in the stables and checking the hay shed. Horseback riders were everywhere. Melancholy cries of "Juliet! Julieeeeet!" echoed across the fields.

Juliet had been missing for two days now, and the last person to see her alive had been beaten into a coma. Was Dex awake this morning? I made my way downstairs, turned on the coffee maker and the kitchen TV. Over the *blurp* and hiss of the brewing coffee, I heard the latest news. Nothing had changed. "The search continues … time is running out … but the missing girl's parents still believe she is alive."

I popped two pieces of bread in the toaster as I watched Midge

LaRouche repeat her heartrending plea. "If you know *anything* about my daughter, please call …"

I tuned her out. There's not a chance your girl's alive, I thought. Your foolish pride may have killed your daughter.

"In related news," the announcer continued, "police found the missing Dexter Gordon, the sixteen-year-old boy wanted in connection with Juliet LaRouche's disappearance. Police say the Chouteau Forest High School student gave Miss LaRouche a ride home from the holiday party where she was last seen."

Interesting. The news reports made it sound like she hitched a ride home with a boy. No mention that they were dating. Did Juliet's parents insist on that careful wording, or was Jace being cagey?

Dexter's photo flashed on the screen. This was a different boy from the beaten, bleeding Dex of last night. He was darkly handsome with a sullen, pouty-lipped sneer. I could see why Juliet might find him attractive compared to the smug pretty-boy blonds in her circle.

My toast popped up. I slathered it with butter, poured myself a cup of coffee, and savored my breakfast at the kitchen table, while the TV announcer showed stock video of the inside of the mall. "Shoppers recognized Dexter Gordon in the food court at the West Forest Mall about nine o'clock last night, according to police sources. The boy was attacked and brutally beaten. He was taken to Sisters of Sorrow Hospital with multiple injuries, including a head injury which has resulted in a coma. He is still unconscious and police are unable to interview him until he regains consciousness."

Juliet's last hope was lying in a hospital bed, I thought. And where was the girl? With her friends? Not after this search. Under a blanket of snow? That was more likely. Did Dex kill her? I didn't know, but I did hear the boy lie to Jace.

Was Jace being pressured to blame the boy for Juliet's disappearance? If so, he'd managed to resist. So far.

The news continued: "Three Forest residents have been arrested in connection with the beating of sixteen-year-old Dexter Gordon at the West Forest Mall. Mall security footage shows the attackers repeatedly kicking and punching the boy. Police say the attack was unprovoked. Charges have been filed against Roger ..."

I switched off the TV, and heard the text chime on my phone. Daisy had texted, *Still want to go to the Olive Garden. Can you take me? You promised.*

I texted back, *Pick you up in half an hour.* But you're not going to like where I'm taking you, missy.

I dressed warmly – too warmly. By the time I stepped out into the crystalline cold, I was sweating. My black Charger was a salt-crusted lump.

On the way to Daisy's house, the sun sparkled on the snow, but it was no longer pristine. The fields had been trampled by searchers and the snow piles along the roadway were slush gray. As the Charger pulled into Daisy's driveway, she ran outside, dressed in her long hooded red coat, black scarf and black boots. She opened the car door and didn't bother with small talk, or even a hello. The frigid air rushed in as she plopped into my passenger seat. When I stopped to turn into the street, Daisy started to put in her ear buds. I put the car in park and grabbed the ear buds.

"Hey!" Daisy said.

"Oh, no. You're not going to listen to music. Not till you see this first." I ignored Daisy's sullen pout and showed her latest TV clip. The announcer said, "As temperatures dip below zero for the second day in a row, hope is running out that sixteen-year-old Juliet LaRouche will be found alive."

"Hear that? Your friend is dead."

"No!" Daisy's eyes were wide and she looked ready to cry. Her voice rose to a shrill denial. "That's not true. She can't be. She can't be."

She was crying, and I didn't care. "Then where is she? They've been searching the Forest for two days now."

"She's hiding at her nana's."

"Her nana's? Where did that come from? You said she was staying at the Minterns."

"I did, but she wasn't there. She has to be at Nana's."

"Why hasn't Nana called the police?"

"She lives at the Willingham. You know where that is?"

"I've been there." The Willingham is a luxurious home for the Forest's richest seniors, and death is a frequent visitor. My death investigator duties brought me there several times. The Willingham is no sad old folks' home. It looks like a luxury hotel, and its services range from assisted living apartments to memory units for people with Alzheimer's.

I turned left toward the Olive Garden – and the Willingham.

"Does Nana have Alzheimer's?" I asked.

"No, she's not that bad. She's a little ditzy, but she knows who Juliet is. Juliet likes to visit her. Sometimes Nana talks about the old days. Most of the time she sleeps and Juliet just hangs. Seeing Nana gets Juliet out of the house and away from her mother."

"Why didn't you tell Juliet's parents that she likes to be with her nana?"

"She needs her privacy."

"She's beyond privacy now. We're going to the Willingham."

"No! I've got to go to the Garden."

"You'll get lunch after we see if Juliet is with Nana. What's wrong with you? Don't you care about your friend?"

"Of course, I care," Daisy said through her tears. "But I know she's okay."

"How do you know that?"

She was red-faced and sniffling. "Because we're like sisters. Like soul sisters. If anything happened to her, I'd feel it." Daisy's tears were nearly shrieks.

"Bull–" I saw the girl's distress and amended it to "baloney. Let's go to the Willingham. Juliet's parents are half-crazed with worry. If you were any kind of a friend, you would have told them by now."

"You don't understand. Juliet's mother has all kinds of stupid plans for her. It's like she's in prison. Her mother tells Juliet what to eat and what to wear and who to see. That's why she had to sneak out to see Dexter. Her mother thought he would ruin her chances to be a DV Queen. It's like the most important thing in the world."

"Only here," I said.

"Huh?" Daisy looked surprised.

"Most people outside the Forest have never heard of the Daughters of Versailles Ball. Those who have think there's something funny about it."

"I don't want to go to the DV, but I don't see why it's funny. It's just a party for friends."

"White, rich friends."

"You're prejudiced against white people," Daisy said.

"I am a white person," I said. The debate ended at the gates of the Willingham. The four-story redbrick building had *Gone with the Wind* columns and park-like grounds blanketed by snow. The front walkway had been shoveled. The grounds were deserted and the parking lot nearly empty.

"What's Nana's name?" I asked.

"Sylvia Du Pres LaRouche." Daisy had finally stopped crying and blew her nose.

I started to park in the front lot, but Daisy said, "There's no point in checking at the front desk. Juliet never signs in as a visitor. She doesn't want her mother to know this is her secret hiding spot. Park around back. The staff keeps a door unlocked so they can smoke by the Dumpster."

I drove around to the back of the building. The Dumpsters were hidden in a high, white-painted fenced enclosure and its gate was slightly open. I could see a door, sheltered by a green canvas awning. "That's it. There," Daisy said. "Park by those evergreens."

I did, then grabbed my purse and followed Daisy across the parking lot, grateful it had been plowed and salted. Even the Willingham's back entrance was impressive. The hall was papered with soft, yellow-and-white striped wallpaper and the walls were hung with landscapes. The only differences between this hall and a pricey hotel were the handrails on the walls and the extra-wide doorways.

"Follow me," Daisy said, and we threaded our way through the deserted halls, past suites with the residents' names on the doors. Occasionally we'd see a nurse or staff member. A twenty-something staffer in a red sweater and black pants pushed a frail, white-haired woman in a wheelchair. Some of the staff nodded at me. No one noticed Daisy.

At last we came to a door with a plaque that read, "Suite 817 – Mrs. LaRouche."

"This is Nana's," Daisy whispered. She opened the door slowly and I heard loud snores. "Nana's asleep. She sleeps a lot. Juliet usually hangs in the chair by her bed."

We tiptoed through a small sitting room with a beige couch piled with needlepoint pillows. The TV was blaring. The walls were covered with photos of Nana and her husband, their children and grandchildren. Over the small wooden table in the kitchenette was a memorial to the dead man. The largest photo showed a tall, good-looking young lieutenant in a naval officer's uniform with a radiant blonde bride in a shoulder-padded wedding dress and veil. In other photos, the same man wore a business suit at an office, posed for family photos, and was a gray-haired executive in a framed newspaper article: "LaRouche Industries CEO Retires at the Top of His Game." Next to that was his framed obituary, dated June 6, 1998.

We passed through the tiny kitchen to a dark bedroom with a hospital bed, a portable toilet and a walker. A waxen older woman in a pink dressing gown snored in the bed, her white hair as fluffy as cotton, her toothless mouth open. Next to the bed, the blue recliner was empty.

The blood drained from Daisy's face. "She's not here. Juliet's not here."

She began searching the room frantically, tossing aside folded nightgowns, dropping papers and magazines on the floor, kicking slippers out of the way, her eyes wide with fear. "She's not here. Juliet's not here. I can't find her backpack. There's no cell phone. Nothing. She's not here. She has to be."

Daisy dropped to her hands and knees and looked under the bed, then jumped up and flung open the bathroom door. The bathroom was empty.

"Where is she?" Daisy shouted.

The old woman stirred in her sleep.

"Sh!" I said. "You'll wake up Mrs. LaRouche."

"Where is she?" Daisy wailed. "She has to be here. She has to be."

I heard footsteps in the distance. I dragged the girl through the halls and out toward the back door. Daisy never stopped weeping.

CHAPTER 10

Wednesday, December 28, 11:37 a.m.

Daisy erupted into hiccoughing sobs in the Willingham hallway. I was sure someone would call security, but we made it to the car and out of the home's grounds.

I parked in the shopping mall lot next door and kept my voice gentle. "Daisy."

The girl continued her noisy tears, snot streaming down her face. Yuck. Daisy pulled another tissue from her purse and blew her nose. She'd been forced to face reality, and it was ugly.

"Daisy!" My voice was sharper. The red-eyed girl looked up and stopped sniffling. "Is there any place else where you think Juliet could be?"

"No." *Sniff.* More tears gathered in Daisy's eyes. I headed them off quickly. "Then show me the secret path by her home."

"I can't!" Daisy wailed. "If her parents find out, she'll get in like serious trouble."

"They don't care if she snuck out to see Dexter. Not any more. All they want is to find their daughter. She's been missing for two days.

They're not going to punish her if they find out about the shortcut. Take me to the secret path."

Daisy switched to her default mode, surly defiance. "And if I don't?"

Time to unleash my inner witch. "Then I'll leave you here and you can walk home."

Daisy looked frightened. "But that's, that's like miles. I'll freeze to death."

"Where does Juliet live?"

"In the old part of the Forest. Even older than where we live. She has one of those really big houses not too far from the Du Pres."

I didn't ask which Du Pres family. The Forest was infested with them.

"What's Juliet's address?"

"She lives on Ondine Terrace. Number six. First house past the stop sign."

"Ondine? For real? That's her street?"

"What's wrong with Ondine?"

"Don't you know who she was?"

"Somebody old and dead."

"Kind of. Ondine was a mythical creature, a water nymph, and she was ..."

Tragic, I started to say, but looked at Daisy's tearful face. I couldn't say it.

"... incredibly beautiful and very independent."

"Like Juliet," Daisy said. I couldn't believe it. The kid was actually listening.

"Right. And like Juliet, she fell in love with the wrong man. He wasn't a Toonerville mechanic, he was a noble, like a duke or a lord. Because Ondine was a nymph, if she fell in love with a man and they had a kid, she would lose her looks and get old and die, just like us. That didn't stop her. Ondine saw this duke and fell in love with him. She didn't care that he was already engaged, or that she'd get old and die."

The girl was still listening. Maybe nobody had ever told her fairy tales. Maybe she thought nymphs were like the Kardashians. "The duke said he'd love her forever. He swore his every waking breath would be a pledge of love and faithfulness."

"That's kinda stupid," Daisy said. "So what happened?"

Nothing good, I thought.

"They got married and had a baby and Ondine started getting old. Her husband got bored and had an affair with another woman, and Ondine found them together."

"What a shit. Did she, like, kill him?"

"Much worse. She cursed him. She told the duke that he'd promised to be faithful with 'every waking breath.' She said, 'As long as you're awake, you can breathe. If you fall asleep, you'll die.' Guess what? He couldn't stay awake and he died."

Daisy looked unimpressed. "I don't see where Ondine has anything to do with Juliet. Juliet's not pregnant."

"So no problem."

"That's what I said." Daisy shrugged. At least she'd stopped crying.

I turned off Gravois into the realm of the super-rich. Through the winter dead trees I glimpsed a Bavarian hunting lodge, a French chateau, and a gray gothic pile with honest-to-God gargoyles, surrounded by acres of snow-frosted woods and towering evergreens.

"Ondine Terrace is the next street," Daisy said. "That's Juliet's house through those trees." I turned and my car slid slightly. Even on a drab winter day, the winding road was scenic.

"That's her place, straight ahead."

The LaRouche house was big, even by Forest standards—four stories of blood-red brick trimmed with white limestone. I got closer, and counted six chimneys before I swerved to avoid a squirrel zipping across the street. As I slowed to a crawl, I saw the architect had added a truckload of useless doodads to the LaRouche house—bulging bay windows, rotundas, a widow's walk, even a bell tower. A half-dozen gables sprouted from the gray slate roof.

"My dad says it's an architectural mess." Why did Daisy slam Juliet's home? Did she need to feel superior to her richer, prettier friend?

"There's certainly a lot of it." There were no cars in the gated courtyard, and I wondered if the LaRouches were searching for their daughter.

"There's the stop sign," Daisy said. "Turn around by her house and come back. You can park by those evergreens so no one will see you. The path is right there."

"I'm not parking in a snowbank. We'll park here on the side of the road. Where's the path?"

Daisy pointed to the snow-covered woods. "There."

My eyes followed her finger. "I don't see it."

"Well, duh," Daisy said. "That's why it's secret."

"Get out and take me to it."

"It's cold." Daisy's whine grated on me worse than her crying.

"If it's cold for you, what do you think it's like for Juliet?" I prayed Juliet wasn't past feeling cold. I hoped she was frolicking with some high school stud.

I saw a trampled path to the right and started toward it. "No! Don't go there," Daisy said. "Nobody uses that path."

"Somebody did. The snow has footprints all over it."

"That's the path the grownups know about. We never take it. Our secret place is down this one."

The wind whipped through my heavy coat as if it was light cotton, and my fingers felt numb in my thick gloves. I pulled my hat down over my ears and my scarf up so only my eyes were exposed to the biting cold, and climbed over the pile of plowed snow along the road.

Daisy followed, grumbling and complaining. I carefully climbed down into and then out of a slippery drainage ditch. I was sweating despite the cold. Dead brown leaves and frozen snow crunched underfoot. At the top of the ditch, I faced a bramble patch draped with dead poison ivy. Behind the thorns and poison was the serene stillness of the Forest.

"Now what?"

"Go around that log," Daisy said, "and you'll see the real path."

I still didn't see it, but my feet felt it. The ground was smoother now. The path was about two feet wide and no footprints disturbed the snow. Maples, oaks, sweet gums, and persimmon trees reached down to pull at my clothes. I walked carefully through the powdery, drifting snow. Once, I stumbled over a rock, but a convenient branch saved me from a fall. The icy wind was blowing harder now and Daisy's whining never stopped.

"How long will it take to get to Juliet's house?"

"About two more minutes. Maybe three," Daisy said.

"Juliet was last seen going into these woods and she never reached her home. We'll keep walking until we get to her house and then we'll turn back."

"Juliet was last seen by Dex. He says she ran into the woods. How do we know he's telling the truth? What if he killed her?" Daisy seemed surprised that last sentence slipped out.

I fought to keep her talking. "Do you think he did?"

"He's from Toonerville. He doesn't like us, and nobody likes him except Juliet. And they had a fight at the party. So he could have killed Juliet."

"If he killed her, where's Juliet's body?"

"I dunno. I'm cold. Can we go now?" The girl's teeth were chattering.

"Let's get to Juliet's house. I can see it past that big oak. Then we can go."

The powdery snow stung my eyes. I blinked back tears and saw something red on the path. "What's that?"

Daisy kicked it with her foot and it clanked. "An old Coke can. We aren't going to find anything. Can we go now?"

"We're almost there."

Crack! A sharp tree branch slapped me in the face, narrowly missing my eye. I stumbled, then brushed against something hanging from a branch near it. Something light blue and soft.

"That's Juliet's!" Daisy said. "That's the velveteen jacket she wore to the party." The girl reached for it.

"Don't touch!" I said. "Leave it for the police." Adrenaline rushed through me, banishing the cold. My heart pounded. I'd stumbled on the first sign of Juliet since she'd disappeared.

A blast of wind nearly knocked me sideways, and the powdery snow swirled, shifted, and revealed sparkling silver in the afternoon sun.

"That's her shoe!" Daisy said. "We went shopping for those high heels. She wore them at the party." She reached for the silver shoe with the delicate ankle straps.

"Don't touch it. The other shoe is next to it."

"He raped her." Daisy was crying again. "He tore off her clothes and raped Juliet. He's an animal."

"We don't know what happened." Something dark blue was draped on a bush. Daisy lunged for it. "That's her dress. Her blue velvet dress. He did rape her!" The girl tried to grab the dress and I stepped in front of her.

"I said don't touch. I'm calling the police. They can investigate this scene."

"But that's her water bottle. See?" Daisy pointed to a pink plastic bottle near the abandoned dress.

"Let the police handle it," I said. "You'll destroy evidence and ruin any chance of finding Juliet."

Beyond the abandoned bottle, the snowy, leaf-covered ground sloped down to a creek. "Stay back, Daisy. Don't touch anything."

I carefully picked my way to the icy edge of the creek. Brown and gray rocks, some as big as basketballs, others small, sharp, and gray, tumbled down the slope into the water where more rocks wore collars of ice on a small muddy beach. The wind howled and blew away more snow, and I saw a mannequin lying in the water. No, not a mannequin. A sculpture. A delicate sculpture of a slender white-skinned girl. She was lying on her back in the cold water, her hair as white as snow, her lips parted, and her blue eyes staring into eternity.

My sluggish brain realized I wasn't looking at a statue. That was a real girl. She was completely nude and frozen solid.

"Juliet!" Daisy screamed.

CHAPTER 11

Wednesday, December 28, 11:55 a.m.

My heart froze when I saw Juliet in the icy creek. The girl looked like a snow sculpture. Her ice blonde hair blended into her snow drift pillow. Her slight body was pale perfection. Snow frosted her cheekbones and her pink-tipped breasts, and dusted her cold blue eyes.

I could see the searchers' tracks in the snow on the other side of the creek. They'd passed right by Juliet. As I watched the wind swirl, I realized the searchers couldn't have seen her snow-covered body until the drifts shifted.

I wanted to find her. But not like this.

The frozen girl was less than five hundred feet from her home. I wondered if someone could see Juliet from the upper windows of her massive mansion.

Daisy's screams broke my concentration. She lunged for the slope down to her friend's frozen body. I grabbed her arm and hung on. I was bigger than Daisy, but the sturdy girl was strong and dragged me through the snow. I tripped her and Daisy landed in the snow with a thud.

"Daisy!" I stepped in front of her, barring the girl's way to the creek. "No. You can't go there."

"She can't be naked like that. People will see her." She tried to shove me aside, but I blocked her again, holding onto a small tree to keep from falling. I couldn't let this hysterical girl ruin the crime scene. I lightly slapped her face and shouted, "Daisy!"

The girl was shocked into silence. "You hit me." More tears, but these were the hot tears of anger.

"Yes, I did. You can't go down there. You'll hurt yourself on the slippery rocks and ruin the crime scene."

"Somebody killed Juliet," Daisy wailed.

"If you want to know who did this, you have to stay away from her body."

Daisy brushed the snow off her coat. "We have to cover her up. The police will see her naked. Everyone will. She'll be so embarrassed."

I was desperate to make the girl understand. "Listen to me. Juliet doesn't care who sees her. She's in heaven. You understand? I'll be the person who examines her here. I'll be respectful and careful. Then we'll cover her and take her away."

Where she'll be autopsied and subjected to indignities I hope you'll never know.

Daisy nodded. Her teeth were chattering again, her lips were gray-blue, and she was having trouble breathing. She was shivering and sweating. She's in shock, I thought. "Let's take you back to my car, so you can warm up. I'll call the police, and we'll get help for Juliet. We shouldn't leave her out here."

The weeping girl was too dazed to protest. I led her back to my black Charger. The car's cold metal door creaked open like a tomb, and I helped the shivering, sweating Daisy lay down in the back seat. I kept the girl in the shock position – flat on her back, with her feet elevated on my big purse to drive more blood to her head. I pulled out the two warm blankets I kept in the trunk and tucked them around the girl. "You're going to be okay. I'll call your parents."

Daisy went paler still and started to sit up. "No! Please! I sneaked out of the house to go to the Olive Garden. They'll kill me." She skipped right past that phrase, not realizing what she'd said. "I'm not supposed to be out in sub-zero weather. Call Rick. You've got his cell. He'll pick me up. Please?"

No trace of her earlier arrogance in that plea. Daisy sounded frightened and much younger than sixteen.

"I promise I'll call Rick. Now lie down."

I walked far enough away that Daisy couldn't hear my phone conversation, but close enough that I could keep an eye on her. Rick answered his cell on the second ring and I blurted out the story. Laid-back Rick was suddenly energized. "Damn, that sucks. Poor little sis. How is she?"

"She's in shock, Rick. She needs you and she's afraid your parents will chew her out because she sneaked out of the house. She's afraid."

"I'm working nearby. I'll be there in ten."

Next I called Jace and gave him the news. "Aw, damn. Poor kid. I'll call out the troops. How's Daisy?"

"She's not doing well. Her brother is on the way."

"He's over twenty-one, right? Because she's a minor and critical to the case. You found that poor girl's body and Daisy identified her. I'll have to question her if she's well enough. You said she's in shock?"

"She's got all the symptoms."

"I'll call an ambulance. I'm on my way."

Jace hung up. I peeked in my car window and thought Daisy might be asleep. Her eyes were closed, her breathing wasn't as labored, and her color looked a little better.

Rick's battered pickup slid around the corner. He roared up, slammed on the brakes behind my car, and jumped out, bringing a cloud of pot smoke with him. His face was creased with worry. "Where's my little sis?"

"Asleep in my car," I said. "The ambulance is on the way. She's afraid to tell your parents."

"Oh, jeez. I'll have a talk with her and get her to come clean. My folks will be pissed, but they'll find out anyway."

The wailing ambulance arrived, interrupting our conversation. After I talked to the two burly paramedics, they gently helped Daisy onto a stretcher and then loaded her into the warm ambulance, where they took her vitals and clamped an oxygen mask over her face. Rick paced up and down outside the doors while they worked on his sister.

I hurried over to see Jace, now parked behind Rick's truck.

"Go ahead. Chew me out," I said. "Tell me I'm an idiot for dragging Daisy here and that her parents will sue my socks off."

"No, you're not an idiot. The boyfriend's still in a coma. The doctors think he'll come out of it, but they're not sure when. You got through to Daisy when we couldn't. If you hadn't found her today, that girl might not have been found for months. Juliet's death is terrible, just about as bad as it can be. The only good part is her parents will be able to bury the daughter they know and love, instead of animal-gnawed bones and scraps of hair. It's cold comfort, but it's all we can do for them. That and find her killer."

Two more cop cars and the Forest crime scene van arrived, and the once quiet street was cluttered with official vehicles. Jace assigned uniforms to handle the traffic, string yellow crime scene tape, and guard the entrance to the secret path.

"Let's hope the cold weather keeps the curious away until we finish this," Jace said. "The tech is here, and we got lucky – it's Sarah 'Nitpicker' Byrne. Let's go see Juliet."

I was so tired I could hardly walk down the snowy path – the cold stole my energy. "Daisy and I made these footprints, Jace. There were no other tracks in the snow before we walked here." The detective followed behind me on the narrow path, crunching carefully in the footsteps Daisy and I had left.

"That's Juliet's velvet jacket on the tree limb." I thought it looked impossibly small twisting in the cold winter sun.

"And those are her high heels."

The silver slippers glittered sadly in the snow.

"That has to be her party dress on the bush," Jace said.

"And her pink water bottle," I said. We were at the lip of the creek now, overlooking Juliet's frozen body. Jace was stunned into silence by the ice queen pillowed in the snow. Finally, he said, "Jesus." The single word was too reverent to be a curse.

He stared for a moment more, then clenched his gloved fists and growled, "That little bastard. When I finish with him, he's gonna beg me to put him back into a coma."

"You think Dex raped her?"

Jace's face was flushed, but I wasn't sure if it was from fury or the biting cold. "She's in the water, isn't she? And her clothes are all over the place."

"Why would Dex rape her outside in sub-zero weather when he had a nice warm car?" I asked. "How did he get her clothes off her? They don't look torn."

"He did it." Jace's face was stone as he repeated those words. "And he's gonna pay."

"Let's get some facts first," I said. "I'll start my investigation. I'll get my kit out of the car."

"You can't go down there," he said. "Not on those slippery rocks. We'll video and photograph the scene, then bring her up."

I followed an angry Jace back to the road. The doors to the ambulance were open and Daisy was sitting up on a stretcher, talking to the two hunky paramedics while her worried brother sat next to her on the ambulance's metal bench.

Jace stalked over. "Rick? How's Daisy? Can she talk?" He seemed genuinely worried about the girl.

Rick seemed totally unaware that he'd perfumed the ambulance with pot. "They say Daisy's stabilized and she wants to talk now. Better do it before Mom and Dad find out. I'm giving you permission. But if she gets too upset, it stops. Understand?"

He was now his sister's fierce protector. Jace nodded, and he and I climbed into the crowded ambulance. I huddled next to Rick on the metal bench and both paramedics watched their patient. Jace sat directly across from Daisy and talked in a soft, friendly voice. "I understand you want to help."

Daisy looked uneasy. Her lower lip trembled and her eyes filled with tears. I leaned forward to catch the girl's teary whisper. "My parents told me to always do the right thing. I should have talked to you before, but they – I mean their lawyer – wouldn't let me. Maybe … maybe if I had, I could have saved Juliet."

Jace cut her off before she started crying. "Juliet was, uh … gone already when you talked to me the first time. But you can tell me what happened the night of the party and then we can find out who killed her. Was Juliet upset at Arabella Du Pres's party?"

"Yes. Really upset."

"What upset her?"

"She had a fight with Dex. He was drunk and bragging that rich girls weren't … weren't …" Daisy was deep pink with embarrassment. Rick shifted and I was afraid he'd shut down the interview.

"Weren't what?" Jace looked her in the eye and smiled. "Please, tell me. This is important."

"I can't say the words."

"Juliet needs you to."

"He said … Dex said poor girls did it better than rich girls, or something like that. And then he said … he said … she had small … she was … small … her breasts were …" The next words poured out in a rush: "She had small tits."

"Did you hear him say that?"

"No, Bella heard about it and told Juliet. She was drunk."

"What was Juliet drinking?"

"Beer. Vodka. Grey Goose, I think. And she had a bag of white stuff."

Jace tensed, but kept his voice soft. "What kind of white stuff? Coke? Heroin? Meth?"

"I don't know, but it was in a big Ziploc bag. Too big to fit in her little purse."

"Who gave it to her?"

Daisy's eyes darted about. "I don't know." I wondered if she was lying. Jace continued his soft questions.

"Were there drugs at the party, Daisy?"

Daisy shifted uneasily and looked frantically around the crowded ambulance until she saw her brother. "I don't want to talk anymore." She dissolved into tears.

"This conversation is over," Rick said, and stood up.

CHAPTER 12

Wednesday, December 28, 12:37 p.m.

I'd been a death investigator for almost twenty years, and I had never encountered a death like Juliet's. I didn't know how to examine a frozen body. I couldn't carry out my usual routine. How could I take a body core temperature and slit the skin to insert the thermometer, when the body was rock hard ice? How could I remove any hairs and fibers frozen to the girl's skin? How much evidence would be lost when Juliet thawed?

I needed help. I called Katie, the Forest's assistant medical examiner.

"I found Juliet," I said. "She's frozen solid."

"Aw, fuck." Katie was silent for a moment. In that brief moment, the sadness and waste of Juliet's death overwhelmed me, and I was afraid I'd cry.

"Wait! *You* found her? You personally?"

"Thanks to Rick's little sister. Daisy showed me the secret path Juliet took to her home. We found her body in a creek about five hundred feet from her house. The searchers passed right by her, but no one could see her until the wind shifted and blew away the snow. She's completely naked."

And beautiful. Stunningly, tragically beautiful. And I'm not going to cry. I'm not, dammit. I'm a professional.

"Was she raped?"

"I don't know." I hated how my voice shook. "I don't know how to do this, Katie. Not a frozen body. That's why I called you."

"I remember one frozen case years ago, when I was a resident. Let's see …" She paused briefly. "You'll need two body bags. Do you have any of those old white ones left?"

"I think there's one in my car trunk. We discontinued them because they were too thin."

"They are, but the white makes it easier to see the hairs and fibers when she defrosts. Put her in the white body bag first, then in the heavy black bag. When she gets here, I'll keep her at room temperature so she'll thaw naturally. What's she weigh? A hundred-ten, a hundred-fifteen pounds?"

"Something like that." I gulped back my tears.

"She'll take about 36, maybe 48 hours to defrost."

Like a piece of meat. I fought against my horror at this bizarre conversation. I'd done many ugly body actualizations – drownings, drug overdoses, decompositions in August – but this one seemed worse.

"I'll have to check her every two hours," Katie said. "The hands and feet will probably defrost first, and then I can get scrapings from under her nails. As the defrosting progresses, I'll draw blood and get fluids, including ocular fluid from her eyes, and seminal fluid, if there is any, in the vaginal vault. Did you see any signs of sexual assault – scrapes, bruises, cuts? Any defensive wounds?"

"I couldn't tell from where I was standing. I was on the bank of the creek and she was about eight feet below on a muddy beach. Jace won't let me do my job. He says I can't go down to the creek bed to examine her. He wants to bring the body up."

"You want to climb down into a slippery, snowy creek in the dead of winter when you've just recovered from six strokes?" I heard Katie's anger and disbelief.

"It's been almost two years. I'm fully recovered."

"Save that bullshit for someone who doesn't know you."

"It's my job."

"To break your leg? Let me guess – this is a typical creek with lots of rocks and loose boulders spilling down to the water. They're covered with snow, ice and frozen mud."

"Right."

"You don't have the balance to go down there. If you slip and fall, you'll mess up my findings. I don't need your blood and DNA mixed in with the victim's and her killer's. I don't need valuable evidence lost in a mudslide. Let Jace and whoever else is there get her. Who's the crime scene tech?"

"Nitpicker Byrne is working this one."

"She and Jace are strong and sure-footed. They can carry her up. Before they move her, stand in a safe place at the edge and take lots of photos, then take more once she's hauled up. Have the body bags open and ready and let them put her in them."

"What form do I use? It's not a suicide, or an apparent natural death."

"What the hell, Angela? What's wrong with you? You sound like a rookie."

"This death is really getting to me."

"Use a standard Body Inspection Form. Be sure to mark any and all injuries, and note anything unusual – including the fact that she's nude. Are her clothes nearby?"

"Tossed all over the place. They're hanging on trees or dumped in the snow."

"Photograph those, too. Exactly where they've landed. I'll check the police video, too, but the location of her clothes is important. Are you sure you're going to be okay?"

"I'll be fine," I said, but my voice shook and I swallowed hard.

"You better be. I'll stop by your house tonight and check on you."

I clicked off my cell, then hauled my death investigator suitcase out of my car trunk and dragged it through the snow. I rolled it swiftly across the plowed street, but the snow, brambles and bushes at the secret path's entrance looked like an insurmountable obstacle. The uniform guarding it lifted my suitcase over the brambles and set it on the path on the other side of the yellow crime scene tape. "Do you need help?" he asked. "Can I carry it to the scene?"

"I can handle it now, thanks." I bumped and dragged the suitcase down the path toward Juliet's body, determined to do this on my own. I slid several times, but I made it. Nitpicker was videoing Juliet's clothes, when she saw me grab a sapling to keep from falling.

"Here, Angela. Let me take that." She grabbed my suitcase.

"I can handle it. I'm not a wimp."

"The way you came back after those strokes, nobody's going to call you a wimp."

"I'm glad you haven't moved Juliet's clothes yet," I said. "I need to photograph them for Katie."

"Help yourself. I'm finishing up. I've done a partial search of the ground and bagged everything."

"Find anything useful?"

She shrugged. "Doubt it. Some trash – a Coke can and some candy wrappers, but they look like they've been here a while."

Juliet's clothes looked like an art installation—the soft, snow-dusted velvet jacket, the silver shoes glittering in the pale winter sun, and the strapless dress spread out on the bush. I took wide shots of the bizarre scene. After I finished the medium shots, I worked on close-ups of each item.

"Where's Jace?" I asked.

"In his car, drinking coffee and warming up before we climb down into that ice-cold creek. It's so damn cold we're working in shifts."

Already, I was bone cold. I tried to ignore it by photographing the girl's clothes. I felt a pang of sadness at the velvet jacket's exquisite details, including the delicate silver filigree buttons.

As I shot pictures of the girl's shoes, I asked, "Find any underwear?"

"Nope, and I don't expect to. I'm guessing she went commando. Lots of young girls do. I did find her purse in a snowdrift." She showed me an evidence bag with a delicate silver purse. "It's just big enough for a cell phone and a lipstick, but there wasn't a cell phone."

"I think the police found the phone in her boyfriend's car," I said.

"I'm pretty sure her water bottle doesn't contain water." She showed me another bag that held the pink plastic bottle with maybe an ounce of clear liquid. "It didn't freeze. It will be opened in the lab when we print it, but I'm guessing that's either gin or vodka."

"Her friend Daisy said she was drinking Grey Goose."

"Vodka then. If you're finished with the jacket and shoes, I'll bag them."

I nodded and Nitpicker put them in brown paper bags. If they were sealed in plastic bags, they'd mildew when the snow on them melted into water. They'd dry out on hangers.

"I'm finished with the dress now, too," I said. I was at the creek's edge and could see the icy body. "I'll photograph the body before you and Jace move it. Katie says it should be double-bagged with a white and a black body bag. I'll have them ready by the time you bring her up."

Nitpicker carefully pulled the blue velvet dress from the bush so it wouldn't tear. "Go ahead. You can use that clear surface there for the body bags."

When she'd cleared the dress fabric from the last twig, she said, "Hello. What have we here?"

Underneath the party dress was a gallon-size plastic Ziploc bag containing a whitish powder. Sarah pulled it out with gloved hands.

"What is that?" I asked.

"Don't know," the tech said. "But it sure is suspicious. I'd better get Jace and tell him."

While Sally left to find Jace, I took dozens of photographs of the frozen girl from the edge of the cliff. Juliet's left arm was flung out and her right arm was frozen to her side. As the powdery snow shifted and swirled around the body, I wondered, did Juliet overdose? Who gave her that suspicious white substance? Was the dead girl raped and murdered, or did she OD?

The cold stung my eyes until they watered. Or maybe those were tears. I was too numb to know any more. My ears ached and my face felt stiff and frozen. At least my iPad was still working. I called up the Body Inspection (Actualization) Form on it and typed in the case number, the time, and checked my thermometer for the ambient temperature – a chilling two degrees.

As I was finishing, Jace and Sarah returned and the tech handed me a steaming foam cup. "I brought you hot coffee. Go warm up in Jace's car while we bring her up. Then I can warm up while you do your death investigation. I showed Jace the white substance. I'm not going to field test it. We'll look at it in the lab. Go on, so we can get started. His keys are in the ignition."

I was grateful for the break. I drank the cup by the time I made my way back to Jace's unmarked car. I poured another cup from the big Thermos on the passenger seat, turned on the engine, and reveled in the blast of warm air. I closed my eyes and drifted off. All too soon, Sarah was knocking on the driver's side window. I opened the door and flinched at the cold.

"My turn." Sarah's gloves, coat sleeves, and boots were wet and muddy, and she had a muddy smudge on her cheek. She was shivering and her teeth chattered. "We got that poor girl out, and I hope I never have to do anything like that again. Good thing I lift weights."

At the scene, I called up the form again. I could type with gloves on and correct the mistakes before I turned in my report. I kneeled down on a third body bag, folded to protect me from the cold. I estimated the girl's weight at a hundred fifteen pounds. Katie would confirm that when Juliet defrosted. I measured her height at five feet two inches, then started with the girl's head. Her hair was too frozen to check her head for lumps. I saw a six-inch-long scrape on the girl's right cheek and near her hairline three half-inch cuts, known as "cut-like defects" in my jurisdiction. From the lack of blood and bruising, I suspect these happened very close to the girl's death, or just after it – postmortem.

The decedent had a thin twelve-inch bruise, a "contusion," on her upper chest from her left breast to her armpit. Both legs were criss-crossed with multiple cut-like defects – I counted eleven – possibly from the brambles and frozen weeds along the path. Her legs were frozen together, but I saw no bruising, contusions or cut-like defects near her sugar-white pubic hair, and none of the telltale thumb-print sized bruises on her hips and thighs that often marked rape victims. There did not appear to be any semen stains on her pelvis, thighs and legs. Her narrow white feet both had quarter-inch blisters on her fifth "little" toes, possibly from the high heels, and her feet were contused, bruised and covered with cut-like defects—ten on her right foot, six on her left, ranging from an eighth of an inch to an inch and a half.

"Jace," I said, "help me turn her over, please."

We were both clumsy and slow from the cold, but we managed to turn the girl. The injuries on Juliet's back side were similar to the front. She had two ten-inch cut-like defects on her bare back, a large bruise five inches wide by three inches long on her round right but-tock, and more contusions and cuts on her thighs and lower legs. I counted and measured them all, as well as the half-inch blisters just above her heels.

"I think those pretty silver shoes must have hurt like hell, Jace." I pointed out the blisters. "Do you think she OD'd on that white powder?"

"No, Juliet was raped by that little son of a bitch. As soon as he wakes up, I'm charging him with felony assault, first-degree murder, and everything else I can think of. I hate rapists – they destroy the innocent."

"I guess you saw a lot of that in Chicago."

"It wasn't in Chicago. It was in my family. My cousin, not much older than Juliet, was raped when her car died on a dark street in the middle of the night. We caught him, but she never got over it. Rapists are the scum of the earth. They deserve the death penalty, every one of them."

Whoa. Jace had convinced himself that Dex had raped Juliet, and his hatred overrode his reason. Nothing I could say would change Jace's mind. He needed the facts from Katie. I believed alcohol and extreme cold had caused this tragedy. They were a dangerous combination. A niggling idea was at the back of my brain.

Jace was still raging about rapists. "Like you said, you're only a DI, not a pathologist, Angela. I'll wait for the report before I charge the little scumbag. Dex killed that innocent little girl, and he's going to pay."

I wasn't sure which was colder, the winter wind or Jace's voice.

CHAPTER 13

Wednesday, December 28, 3:18 p.m.

A wild-eyed Prentice LaRouche confronted Jace and me in the middle of the street. Midge, red-eyed and wringing her hands, hovered near her husband like a lost soul.

"He did this! He killed our little girl."

After the morgue transport van had left with Juliet's frozen body, Jace and I had planned to go to the LaRouche home to tell the couple the sad news. Instead, their Range Rover tore down the street and squealed to a stop in front of us. I jumped back toward the curb to avoid getting hit, Jace grabbing my elbow to steady me.

"Are you okay?" he asked.

Before I could answer, Prentice, nearly crazed with rage, vaulted out of the driver's seat and marched over. Midge climbed slowly out of the luxury vehicle, holding onto the door post. She was so crushed and broken she could barely stand.

"I demand answers!" he shouted. "Why wasn't I informed that you'd found my daughter? Why did I have to hear this from a neighbor?"

"We were on our way to inform you, Mr. LaRouche," Jace said. "We're sorry for your loss."

"Sorry! You should have called me the moment you found her."

"We make notifications in person, sir, and our first priority was to process the crime scene."

"NO! *You* work for me! Your first priority is to tell me. I'm her father." Prentice was spitting he was so angry.

"Mr. LaRouche." Jace's voice was gentle. "I'm a father, too. I can't imagine the pain you and your wife must be feeling, but I don't work for you."

"I pay your salary!"

"Your taxes *help* pay my salary, but I work for the city of Chouteau Forest. For all the citizens. My job is to process the crime scene, then find your daughter's killer and bring that person to justice."

"I already know who killed her, and you do, too." Prentice was shouting. His wife's heart-wrenching sobs were a sad background for his tirade. "That son of a bitch Dexter Gordon murdered my little girl. We didn't want her going out with that trash. We refused to let her see him, but she sneaked out of the house. If she'd stayed with her own kind, this would have never happened. Why hasn't he been arrested?"

"He's in a coma in the hospital. And I need proof, Mr. LaRouche." The same detective who was ready to slap the cuffs on Dexter a moment ago was now a model of restraint. Maybe he didn't like being ordered around.

Prentice's voice rose to a roar. "I demand that you arrest him this instant. My daughter deserves justice."

"And the best way to get justice is to have the evidence. The medical examiner has to do his job first."

Midge screamed as if she'd been shot. "You're going to cut up my baby?" She staggered back and landed in a snow pile. I rushed over and helped the weeping woman stand. "Why? Why do you have to cut up my baby?" Midge sobbed and I held the grieving mother and rocked her. Prentice stared at his wife, his face expressionless.

"I'm sorry," I said. "It's the only way to know what happened to Juliet."

"Is it true she wasn't wearing any … she didn't have on any …" Midge forced herself to say the next sentence. "Her clothes were gone?"

"Yes," I said.

"That's proof she was raped!" Prentice yelled. "How much more do you need?"

Midge collapsed against me, howling as if she'd been set on fire.

"Mr. LaRouche, let's get your wife home and call a doctor for her," I said. Jace and I guided Midge to the Range Rover. I was surprised how light Midge felt. The sturdy, vigorous woman of Tuesday morning was now old and shrunken. She lay back in her seat, tears flooding her cheeks.

"Where do we go to identify my daughter?" Prentice asked.

Jace opened Prentice's door for him. "She's been formally identified, sir. Please, take your wife home and get her the medical attention she needs."

"I'll ruin those worthless people! I'll destroy his greaser father. I'll take his business. He won't have a nickel to his name when I'm through with him. The Gordons' lives will be over, just like my daughter's."

He turned to Jace. "And you. I'll have your job." With that parting shot, Prentice drove the short distance to his home.

I watched the LaRouches' wrought iron gates slide open and swallow the distraught parents. I sighed and reached for my DI suitcase. "That was purely awful."

Jace helped me lift the suitcase into my car trunk. "I still believe that boy raped and murdered her, Angela, but I need the DNA evidence before I can charge him. And he's going to be charged as an adult. I expect Prentice will call the police and make my life a misery."

"It's going to take about two days to thaw the body," I said. "I still don't think he's guilty. If he's not, can Dex be charged with manslaughter because he didn't make sure Juliet was safely home?"

"No, but I might get him on culpable negligence. And Dexter's family can be charged with impeding an investigation and lying to the police. They're the ones who ordered him to go to his grandparents' house in St. Louis. I can get him and his parents on obstruction of justice and false information. And I see a civil suit because if his family had been honest, the girl might have been found and saved."

I thought the girl was probably dead by the time Prentice LaRouche pounded on the Gordons' front door.

"Juliet's family is equally guilty," I said. "The LaRouches withheld important information, too. They never told you she snuck out to go to the party with Dexter. And what about the kids who got drunk at Bella Du Pres's house and possibly used drugs? What about charges against her parents? They definitely knew alcohol was being served and they may have turned a blind eye to drugs."

"Uh, I'll have to think about that. You going to file your report?"

"Heading home now to warm my fingers and then send it in." Jace slapped the side of my Charger like a horse's rump and waved good-bye.

I drove home, disappointed that the new detective was going to give in to the Forest's first families like everyone else. I was worried about Dex, a blue collar boy in a rich man's world. Soon the news would be all over the Forest, and the first families would turn into a lynch mob.

I dragged myself up my driveway, then took a long hot shower to warm up. I wrapped myself in my comforting brown robe, fixed myself a hot chocolate, and settled in to write Juliet's report. It took me longer than usual. Images of Juliet's frozen beauty played in my mind on an endless loop, and I cried as I e-mailed her photos to the ME's office.

I was too involved with this case. I knew that, but I couldn't believe Dex killed Juliet. Not yet. Not until all the possibilities were investigated. Did an angry Brock follow Juliet to the path and kill her in a jealous rage? What is that mystery bag of white powder? Juliet had been drinking all night. Did she die of alcohol poisoning? It was too easy to blame a Toonerville kid. We'd already lost Juliet. Did Dex have to be another victim?

I remembered Rick DeMun talking about the system of shortcut paths used by the Forest teens. Maybe they held the answer.

I called Rick. "How's your little sister?"

"She's in bad shape. This is the first time someone her age, someone she knows, has died. At sixteen, dying is something that happens to old, old people, like our Great-Aunt Violet, and she was all fixed up in a casket. But poor Daisy saw her best friend stark naked in a frozen creek. She can't stop crying. Mom wants her to see a counselor, and that may be the best way to handle it. Daisy definitely needs help."

"How much trouble is she in?"

"Believe it or not, the kid got off easy. Mom had already heard about Juliet and she was so glad Daisy was alive she practically carried her inside. She fussed over her for hours before she got mad and punished her."

"Is she grounded?"

"No, Mom hit Daisy in the wallet. Daisy has to pay for her car repairs with her own money. That's about five hundred dollars."

"That's gotta hurt."

"It will cut into her plans to buy more clothes, but she'll sweet talk Grandma into getting them for her for her birthday in March. Mom said Daisy could go out with her friends, but there are more restrictions – she made Daisy promise that she'd tell her when she left the house and she has to take a selfie wherever she is so Mom can check that she's really there."

"So, not too bad."

"That's the advantage of being the baby of the family. I would have been grounded until I graduated. But I think it's a good idea to let Daisy go out with her friends. Maybe she'll stop crying. If she asks you to drive her to the Olive Garden, will you take her?"

"Your mom will let her out this soon?"

"Don't worry about Daisy. She'll know how to persuade Mom to let you drive her. She'll look all sad-eyed and Mom will cave. So promise me you will."

"Deal. Now I have a question for you, Rick. You said there was a network of paths in the Forest that the kids took. Could you show them to me? I'll buy you lunch."

"You don't have to bribe me, Angela. I'll be happy to show you if you give me enough hot coffee and more of that banana bread. But can you walk in the woods on slippery, snowy paths?"

"I did fine walking the path during Juliet's death investigation. If I don't have to roll a suitcase, I can make it, though I may lean on you if it gets too icy."

"At your service."

"And I'll not only feed you coffee and banana bread, I'll give you your own loaf to take home." I knew the gentle pothead had a perpetual case of the munchies.

"Totally not necessary, but I'll take it. It's supposed to warm up to thirty degrees tomorrow. I don't have a job until eleven. I'll be at your house at nine o'clock. Dress warm."

After Rick hung up, I settled into my living room and clicked on the evening news. The main local story was almost unbearable: Juliet's death, with photos of the lost girl's otherworldly beauty, followed by footage of the lonely path where she died, and a high school photo of Dexter that made the boy look like a scowling thug. A reporter tried to talk to the LaRouches but couldn't get past their black wrought-iron gate covered with a huge black silk wreath.

Another story showed warmly dressed picketers gathered outside the hospital entrance, some holding candles, others with signs that said, JUSTICE FOR JULIET.

"Arrest the killer now," demanded a solemn-faced senior newscaster on a "TV-torial" following the news. "Let Dexter Gordon wake up in custody and be tried as an adult. His punishment needs to start now."

I switched off the TV in disgust, and heard a vehicle rattling up my driveway. I looked out the window. Katie!

My friend burst in with a flash of cold, a box of chocolate truffles, and a hug for me.

"Want some wine?" I asked.

"Make it coffee. Juliet's my case and I have to go back and check on her in another hour and a half."

I measured out coffee and poured water into the coffee maker. "I thought the boss would want this high profile case."

"Too much work. I have to check on her every two hours. Besides, he doesn't want to be the guy who carved up the LaRouches' beautiful girl."

"How are you going to get any sleep when you're checking on the body every two hours?"

"I'll find a cot in one of the doctors' lounges at SOS. Monty's nephew is still here, so it's not like I'm missing anything. And by the way, you don't look much better than some of the folks in my cooler."

"It's this old robe."

"The hell it is. You're pale and exhausted – and you look like you've been crying. You're too wrapped up in this case."

I was grateful the coffee maker gave a final hiss. I poured two mugs of black coffee and brought them into the living room.

"Have a chocolate," Katie said. It was a command, but the sugar and caffeine rush helped restore me.

"Did you see the news, Katie? Dex is being railroaded for rape and murder, and there's no evidence he did it. You haven't even started.

No one's looking for reasons why Juliet died. She was probably drunk when she ran out of Dex's car into the woods. We found what looks like vodka near her body."

"I haven't done a blood alcohol test. She's not defrosted enough."

"And you haven't done a tox screen. The lab hasn't tested that big bag of white powder found in the bushes. Juliet got in a fight with Brock Sedgwick. She could have been sexually assaulted by him."

"Except there don't seem to be signs of assault."

"Maybe it was consensual," I said. "Revenge sex because she was mad at Dex. And then she laughed at Brock or they had a fight and he murdered Juliet or left her to freeze in the woods."

"It's happened before, especially with teenagers. That fifteen-year-old who was strangled in the woods last summer laughed at her boyfriend when he couldn't get it up, and he killed her."

"Daisy also said Bella's mother made Juliet cry. She claims she doesn't know why, but there's more to that story. Bella's mother gave Juliet some kind of gift that calmed the girl but still made her unhappy. What was it?

"And what goes on along the secret network of paths in the Forest? Rick is going to show me some tomorrow."

"Be careful, Angela. This is a hot topic in the Forest and it's not your job to investigate Juliet's death. You could lose your job for this stunt."

I stared into my cooling coffee. "I know. It's bad enough that Juliet is dead. I have to stop another tragedy. A blue-collar kid like Dex will be ruined if he's even charged with Juliet's murder."

CHAPTER 14

Thursday, December 29, 9:10 a.m.

"Man, this banana bread is good." Rick spread half a stick of butter on his third thick slice.

The Forest's handyman was praising his snack in my coffee-scented kitchen. "It's way better than my mom's. What makes it so good?"

"It's a secret." It was, too. I'd bought six loaves at a charity bake sale. I defrosted the last loaf this morning so Rick could take it with him.

He finished the buttery banana bread in four bites, then took a final gulp of coffee. "Ready for our path tour? We can take my truck. I cleaned it in your honor."

"Sure." I shut the door and stepped into the bright morning sunshine. "After several bone-chilling days," I said, "it feels almost like spring."

Rick wasn't wearing a hat, and his long brown hair was pulled into a ponytail. "It's twenty-eight, according to the radio. Much easier for us to go walking. The snow won't melt but you won't freeze your ears off."

"Did that yesterday." I was surprised when I climbed into Rick's blue truck. Not only was it neat, it smelled like a bakery.

"Do I smell vanilla?"

"Yep. Ozium."

I laughed. From my work, I knew Ozium was the potheads' preferred air freshener.

"Didn't want you to get a contact high while we're working." Rick carefully stowed his loaf of banana bread under his seat, put the truck in gear and rolled down my drive.

"How's Daisy?" I asked.

"Cried all night. Mom stayed with her – she's worried sick. She offered to take Daisy out, but she won't be seen with Mom."

I smiled. "At least that's normal behavior for a teenager."

Rick shrugged. "I guess. I was gonna give her a toke to help her mellow out, but Mom would kill me. When Daisy's not crying she's on the phone to Bella. They actually call each other."

"You mean talk instead of texting? That's really old school."

"Guess you can't cry together when you text. I wish the LaRouches would hold the funeral. The kids need an outlet for their grief."

"Poor Juliet isn't even defrosted yet," I said. "That's going to take maybe two days, and then there's the autopsy."

"I know. They all know why there's the long wait. That makes it somehow worse. I hate to sound like one of those stupid advice doctors, but once Juliet's buried, they can get on with their lives."

"Maybe they shouldn't, Rick. Not yet. It's a terrible lesson, but it's how teenagers learn death is real."

End of lecture, I told myself. Rick knows this.

"Don't be surprised if Daisy texts you this afternoon and wants to go to the Olive Garden," he said.

"I'll be more than glad to take her."

"Any word on the Toonerville kid they're blaming?"

"Last I heard, he's still in a coma," I said.

"Do you think he offed Juliet?"

"No, I think he's guilty of being a Toonerville outsider, and his parents gave him incredibly stupid advice. When Juliet's dad showed up at their door, they made Dex hide in the basement and then told him to run to his grandparents' home in St. Louis."

"Why?"

"They believed because he was a Toonerville kid, he'd get blamed."

"Well, they were right, but when he ran he looked even guiltier. I hate to see another kid's life ruined."

"I'm hoping this path tour will help clear him. We need to give the police someone else to look at, and Juliet had a fight with another boy the night she disappeared. He could have left the party at the same time and waited for her on the path by her home."

"All the kids use them," Rick said. "It's the best way to get around the Forest without the grownups seeing you or your car. Besides, I like walking in the woods. I started when I was six years old."

"Your parents liked the outdoors?"

Rick laughed. "Hardly. I had a Swedish nanny when I was a kid."

"Wow!"

"If you're thinking a blonde in a string bikini, my mother wasn't that stupid. Annah was a lovely lady, but old enough to be my grandmother. She'd take me for long walks after school and on weekends. Annah knew these woods better than most locals. Even after she went back home, I kept the habit of walking because … uh, my parents are good people, but we don't get one another. I think they picked up the wrong baby at the hospital."

"Rick!"

"I feel sorry for them. Most of my friends are stockbrokers, doctors, and lawyers. My parents got stuck with a hippie throwback."

"With a successful contracting business."

Rick shrugged. "It's too blue collar. They'd rather have a hard charger for a son, but at least I've stayed out of jail. Ah, here's the entrance to my favorite path. You have to see where I used to hang."

I realized we were on Gravois Road, the main thoroughfare through the Forest.

"Different groups of kids staked out their own paths. You can just see this one through those trees." He pointed at a stand of oak along the side of the road, and pulled his truck over. "Oaks keep their leaves in the winter. This used to be the road to reefer madness."

He grinned at me. I climbed out of the truck and he helped me across the snowy culvert. "This path should be big enough for both of us."

I followed him along a winding trail. We passed the ruins of an abandoned farmhouse, little more than snow-covered piles of wood. "On the other side of that house, the path ends in a sort of bowl."

Walking was easy on the wide path. A bird was singing, but when our footsteps crunched on the snow-crusted gravel it flew away.

"There it is!" Rick pointed to a bowl-shaped depression ringed by towering trees. "We used to sit on those big rocks and get high. It was nice and shady in the summer. The potheads hung out here – and they still do. The nerds were closer to the Academy, and the serious users were way back in the woods behind Reggie Du Pres's house. You grew up in the Forest, Angela. Why don't you know about the paths?"

"I was never one for the great outdoors."

"Neither is my sister, but she still takes the paths."

"I went to the Academy, but I didn't hang out with most of the kids. My parents worked for Old Reggie." The kids didn't associate with the daughter of servants.

"Oh. That sucks."

"Not really. I'd rather read a book." That's what I told myself, anyway.

I broke the uncomfortable silence. "The path that runs behind Juliet's house – what kind of kids use it?"

"When I was growing up, that was mainly where the straight kids hung out and smoked cigarettes. There's an old stone spring house hidden back there, and some kids used it to have sex."

"What's a spring house?"

"It's a little building over a natural spring. In the old days, before people had refrigerators, a spring house kept their drinking water clean – kept out the dead leaves and raccoons. They'd also store their butter, meat, and milk there. That could be where Juliet met up with Dex, though they may have gone old school and used his car, or possibly her family's pool house."

I remembered Daisy telling me, *our secret place is down this one.*

"Could you show me the spring house?"

"Can we go there? Didn't the police tape off that path?"

"I think that part of the investigation is over. If there's a problem, I'll call Detective Budewitz."

Five minutes later, Rick was on Juliet's street, parked in the same spot that I had been parked in yesterday. The street entrance to the path was now a shrine to the dead girl, heaped with teddy bears, Mylar balloons, flowers, and homemade posters decorated with hearts and photos of Juliet.

The yellow crime scene tape fluttered in the light breeze, but no police officer guarded the entrance. Rick helped me past the brambles and winter-dead poison ivy. At the creek where Juliet's body had been found were more tributes.

"This is where you and Daisy found her?" Rick said.

I nodded, afraid I'd start crying again. I looked past the pile of tributes and saw a heart-shaped wreath of pink silk roses floating on the spot where Juliet's body had been. The wreath was tied to a thick pink ribbon held down with a massive stone.

We stood in silence for a long moment. "Poor girl. Poor little girl." Rick shook his head. "If you want to go to the spring house, it's past Juliet's house, about a quarter of a mile. Can you walk that far?"

"I'm fine, and not too cold."

This part of the path was not as well used. We trudged through the snow and passed the backs of two massive mansions and a snow-covered tennis court.

"That's Juliet's house." Rick pointed to the four-story brick building, which was surprisingly plain at the back. All the curtains were closed. "If you go a little farther, you can see the spring house down in that hollow."

At first, I thought it was another gray rock jutting out of the ground. But as we walked closer, I saw a flat-roofed gray stone structure about the size of a tool shed in a hollow by the creek. The spring house was covered with green moss and someone had partially repaired the old wooden door.

Rick helped me down to the spring house. I slid slightly in the snow, but his strong arms kept me from falling. Rick pulled open the heavy door and it made a cold, rusty squeak.

Inside, the windowless building was dark and cold as a tomb. The damp chilled my bones. The room stank of cigarettes and was barely big enough for the stained mattress on the floor. Stubbed out cigarettes, empty matchbooks, junk food bags and fast food wrappers littered the floor.

"Do you think Juliet and Dex had sex on that mattress?" I couldn't picture the romantic Juliet making love in this gloomy stone room.

"They could have brought their own bedding in a picnic basket," Rick said. "I've heard stories where guys actually shoveled out the trash, then lit a few candles. This could be romantic if you're sixteen and horny. See. Look at all the melted candles on the ledge."

Dozens of fat candles in a rainbow of colors lined a wide ledge. Most were wax puddles, but a few could still be lit.

"Maybe." Did Brock meet Juliet on the path to her house, and try to persuade her to go to the spring house for sex?

In that case, why did she strip off her clothes by the creek?

CHAPTER 15

Thursday, December 29, 10:29 a.m.

"Damn it, Angela, I can't believe we missed this," Jace said. "That's just shoddy police work."

The detective was pacing up and down on the path, beating himself up. I'd called Jace about the spring house after Rick and I had explored it. Then I'd made sure Rick left for his eleven o'clock job, telling him, "I'll catch a cab home."

I didn't have to wait long for Jace to show up, but I didn't think he'd stop berating himself. "I've slipped since I moved here from Chicago. I'm getting lazy."

"It's not your fault," I said. "You aren't from around here. I grew up in the Forest, and I didn't know about the spring house. Neither did Sarah the tech."

Jace refused to let himself off the hook. "I should have gotten off my lazy rear end and walked the rest of the path."

I shrugged. "You still wouldn't have seen it. From the path, it looks like a big rock. Sarah's on her way and she's gonna have her work cut out for her."

We heard crunching on the snowy path, and there was Nitpicker Byrne, lugging her case. The tech wasn't bundled up quite as much as she'd been for Juliet's death scene. The zaftig blonde's hair changed every time I saw it. This time, she sported a festive green. Last time, it had been bright blue.

Jace helped Sarah with the bulky case and the two climbed down the hill while I stayed on the path. I saw Sarah look inside the spring house and groan. "Jeez, this is a stone Dumpster. How much do you want me to bag and tag?"

"I need everything," Jace said.

"Everything?"

"Sorry, Sarah. It can help me eliminate suspects, or catch them in a lie."

"But some of this junk is old."

"Unless I have a print on a dated register receipt, I don't know how long the stuff has been here," he said. "If there's a suspect, I want him to say he was never in the spring house. Then, if his prints are on that chip bag, we've got him."

"Unless he handled the bag prior to it being taken to the spring house."

"His lawyer can argue that," Jace said.

"You know it's unlikely I'll get prints off this porous stone."

"I know. But if some candle wax was spilled on the stone, a plastic print could be left in the wax. Take those candles, too. Prints could be in the wax."

"Okay, but there are gonna be some disappointed love birds when the weather warms up. Collecting and bagging these butts and trash is going to take the rest of the day. You'll have more DNA than a hot sheet motel. Do you want me to run it all?"

"Let's wait until after the autopsy," Jace said. "If Katie doesn't find any signs of sexual assault, or if the vic died of exposure, you may not have to process this trash heap." He looked apologetic. "I know it's a pain in the ass, and I'm asking a lot, but I've spent many an hour processing cans, butts, wrappers, and worse."

"I'm not complaining, just trying to give you what you want. I want the bastard who killed that little girl as much as you do." Sarah opened her case and started working, and Jace rejoined me back on the path.

"Do you need me to stay," I said, "or can I go home? I can call a cab."

"I'll take you. You're not that far away."

Jace's unmarked Charger was parked on the other side of the shrine to Juliet. We both stood before the sad collection of stuffed animals and wilting flowers for a moment. I saw new bouquets had been added since this morning, along with a miniature pink teddy bear.

On the ride home, I asked, "Any new information from Katie?"

"It's looking less and less like the vic was assaulted," he said. "She didn't find any defensive wounds on her hands, or any fingernail scrapings.

"If Juliet wasn't raped, that will be some comfort for her parents."

"Cold comfort, pardon the phrase. We'll know more when Katie can check for semen. There's no word yet on the blood alcohol level."

"What about the big bag of white powder?" I asked.

"Don't know about that, either. The lab's backed up."

The snow was starting to melt a little when Jace dropped me off at home about twelve-thirty. I made more coffee, then warmed up some tomato soup and fixed a salad – the trek in the cold had made me surprisingly hungry. As I was rinsing my dishes and putting them in the dishwasher, my cell phone chimed. I had a text from Daisy, *Will you take Bella and me to the Olive Garden? Bella's at my house.*

I texted back, *On my way.*

Rick had been right. Daisy did want to go out, and she'd persuaded her mother to let me drive her. I was glad to take the girls. I needed more information.

Daisy and Bella were waiting at the front door of the DeMun house, and hurried out as soon as they saw my car. The girls seemed more subdued today, and a little older. Daisy wore a raccoon mask of eye makeup and a dark green coat. Her brownish hair was pulled into a high ponytail. Round-faced Bella looked chunky in her furry boots and three-quarter-length coat. Most of her hair was hidden by a gray knit cap.

The girls greeted me, then climbed into the back seat as if I was a chauffeur. I felt a burst of annoyance, then decided to cut them some slack. They both looked like they'd been crying; their eyes were red and raw. Daisy had bruise-like marks under her eyes, and I wondered if she'd gotten any sleep.

As I put the car in gear, Daisy said, "Wait! I have to take a selfie in your car and send it to Mom. Then she's okay if I go."

"Gawd, that's like being a prisoner," Bella said.

"She's making me crazy. She wants proof every time I say I'm going anywhere. I have to take another selfie at the Olive Garden when we get there and then when we leave for home. My brother says I got off easy for sneaking out of the house, but I didn't. I have to pay for my own car repairs."

Daisy snapped two cell phone photos of her and Bella in the back seat.

"Let me see," Bella said. "Don't use that one. It makes my nose look big. Not that one, either. My hair looks awful. Take another."

The girls were oblivious to me, but I waited patiently. They had information and I was determined to get it. Daisy snapped more selfies and this time, Bella approved one. "Ready, ladies?"

"Yes. You can go now," Daisy said. "Hurry up. We're gonna be late."

I didn't hold you up taking selfies, I thought, but bit back those words. Teenagers are annoying. Deal with it.

I kept my voice sympathetic. "How are you, Daisy? Rick said you didn't sleep last night."

"Every time I'd close my eyes, I'd see Juliet in the creek, covered with ice and I'd start shivering like I was freezing. It was horrible."

"Did you take pictures of her in the creek?" Bella asked.

"No! It was too awful. I wanted to cover her up and Angela wouldn't let me. Juliet was naked. If I took pictures, everyone would see her like that."

I turned onto Gravois Road, heading for the highway. Daisy was still talking about her lost friend. "Juliet's like the only dead person I've ever known. It hurts to think about her. Every time I start to remember she's dead, I cry. Mom says it will get better and the bad stuff will fade away in time. She said you lost your husband, Angela, and you got over it."

I felt as if Daisy had stabbed me. My hands gripped the steering wheel to control my anger. I knew people talked about Donegan's untimely death, but I hated that the man I loved was part of a casual conversation. "I won't ever get over losing my husband. Ever. It's been almost two years. But it's starting to hurt a little less. I've never lost a friend like you have, Daisy, but I imagine it will be painful for a long time, and then the pain will start to fade and things will get better."

"Not for me," Bella said.

I looked at the chunky brunette in the rear view mirror, then glided onto I-55. The Olive Garden was two exits away.

"Why?"

Bella started crying.

"What's wrong, Bella?" I asked. "Are you okay?"

"You can tell me." Daisy's voice was soft with sympathy. "What's wrong?"

"Everything. Now that Juliet's gone, Mummy says I can be the DV Queen." Bella's voice rose to a wail. She was crying for herself, not for Juliet.

"Mummy made Daddy put up the extra money so I could be Queen. It's another twenty thousand dollars and she said it would be an investment in my future. I didn't even want to be a stupid Maid."

A Ford F-150 pickup blasted my car and swung around us.

"I'd rather have the money," Daisy said.

"Me, too," Bella said. "Now I have to go to lunch with a bunch of creak-a-sauruses at the club."

I assumed that was the Forest Women's Club. Bella's tears had dried up in her outrage.

"The creak-a-whats?" Daisy asked.

"The old ladies who run the DV Selection Committee. They hang out at the Club. They're about a hundred and ten years old and Mummy says they're important. They decide who gets to be Maids and who's Queen."

"I'd refuse to go." Daisy stuck out her chin.

"I did! Mummy said if I don't go, she'll take my car. In fact, she took it now. She said that would" – Bella's voice rose to a precise, prissy tone – "'Give you a taste of what life will be like if you don't make the cut, young lady.'"

She was back to her normal voice now. "I meet with the DV committee this Saturday, and I have to be nice to them. But I still don't get my car back until the wrinklies say yes. Mom also said I could get a new iPhone if they agree and this one is like prehistoric. I'm embarrassed to use it."

"Does your mother know how you feel about being Queen at the Daughters of Versailles Ball?" I asked.

"Of course she fuckin' knows." Bella savored that F-word. "Nobody wants to be part of it. Mummy says she's making these sacrifices for my future. Daddy has to spend money and she's working almost every morning at the Savant Shop to suck up to the old ladies who run the DV committee."

"Ew. I hate that place," Daisy said.

"I do, too," Bella said. "It's like a junk shop."

The Savant Shop was a pricey resale shop where the Forest first families donated their knickknacks and dead relatives' outdated designer dresses. The proceeds went toward the Chouteau Forest Women's Club scholarship fund.

Bella pounded the back of my seat in frustration. "I hate her! I hate her! I hate the fucking DV Ball. And now I have to do it." The girl's face was red with fury.

This was the opening I had been waiting for. "Maybe not, Bella. There may be a way out. At your party, your mother said something to Juliet that upset her. What was it?"

"See, that's what I'm talking about! Mummy was jealous of Juliet because Juliet was perfect. Mummy didn't want her to be the DV Queen, so she told Juliet she was fat."

Fat – the deadliest insult in the female teen world. Now I understood those tears Juliet supposedly shed at the party.

"Mummy told Juliet she had a fat ass."

Daisy brayed a harsh laugh. "Your mom said that? About Juliet? Has she looked at her own ass? She's like what, a sixteen?"

"She's a size fourteen," Bella said. "But that's bad enough. Most stores here don't even carry fourteens. She'd have to buy clothes that big in Toonerville, and she won't shop there. Mummy special orders her clothes from a catalogue cause she's so fat."

I dragged the subject back to Juliet. "So your mother's remarks about Juliet upset her?"

"Upset? Juliet was in hysterics. I was glad the music was so loud no one could hear her. Mummy was downstairs in the kitchen, stuffing her face again. She said if Juliet would calm down, she could fix the problem."

"What did your mother do?" I was determined to get this story.

"She has this fat-busting supplement from her trainer. Mummy's definitely a chunkster and this stuff is supposed to help her lose weight."

"Does it?" Daisy asked.

"Who knows? Mummy talks about losing weight, but she goes on a diet for like two days and then eats a box of chocolate truffles."

I was desperate for this information. "So your mother has a fat-busting supplement."

"A whole tub of it. She gave Juliet a lot in a big plastic bag and told her to drink six scoops a day in cold water and she'd lose that weight in a week or two – and if that didn't work, she'd give Juliet more."

"What color is the supplement?"

"White."

"What's it called?" I asked.

I saw movement in the rear view mirror. Bella shrugged. "I don't know. She keeps it in the kitchen."

We were at the Olive Garden exit now, and I put on my blinker.

"When will you pick us up?" Bella asked.

"Text me when you're ready," I said. "Do you want to go tomorrow, too?"

"Yes!" the girls said together, as I pulled in front of the restaurant.

"Then text me the name of that fat-burning supplement. That's your ticket for tomorrow's ride."

CHAPTER 16

Thursday, December 29, 4:45 p.m.

The text was five words, *Rad Rip Pre-Workout Performance Supplement.*

It wasn't signed, but I knew it came from Bella. I'd taken Daisy home, then dropped Bella at her house about half an hour ago. She'd promised to text me "as soon as I can look in the kitchen cabinets without Mummy watching me."

Bella's text launched a flurry of my own. I texted Katie and Jace, *The bag of white powder may be a weight loss supplement called Rad Rip Pre-Workout Performance Supplement. Lydia Du Pres made Juliet cry at the party when she called her fat. She gave the Rad Rip to the girl for her "weight problem." Those are probably Lydia's prints on the bag.*

Then I started my own internet search. At first, I saw effusive praise for Rad Rip. Dozens of muscle heads declared the pre-workout powder "really makes me feel amped up." "Rad Rip gives me more pumps." One poet wrote, "The fat melts away and I'm amped for the day."

Scientists and investigative journalists explained why the bodybuilders were rarin' to go. Researchers in both US and Europe had tested the powder and discovered Rad Rip contained "amphetamine-like compounds." Those in the scientific know declared it was "highly dangerous."

Rad Rip's manufacturer swore the popular weight loss powder was perfectly safe, but stores and gyms pulled it off their shelves and refused to carry it. I suspected anything was sold in the wild outposts of the World Wide Web. Sure enough, I discovered Rad Rip tubs with "40 servings" were on sale for $34.95. The fine print warned the powder had a high caffeine content, but there was no mention that users would be amped on amphetamines.

What if Juliet had taken this dangerous powder?

I called Katie at the medical examiner's office. "I got your text," she said. "You've saved us a lot of work on that powder."

"Did you get a chance to research Rad Rip?" I asked.

"Not yet, I had to post that poor bastard who drove into a tree."

"I'll show you what I found. That stuff is scary."

"Come on over," she said.

I gathered the printouts about Rad Rip, slipped into my coat, and carefully made my way to my car. The snow was melting just enough to be slippery. By nightfall, when the temperature dropped back into the twenties, it would refreeze.

I was in a hurry to show Katie my Rad Rip research and wanted to floor the gas pedal, but I couldn't risk an accident. Traffic was light and I was at the ME's office behind SOS Hospital in ten minutes.

I found Katie in her closet-sized office, frowning at her computer keyboard, her brown hair oily and her suit rumpled. "You look tired," I said. "You getting any sleep?"

"Not really. I'm still checking the girl every two hours. I packed a bag and I shower and sleep at the hospital."

"Wait till you see this," I said. "You won't believe what's in that Rad Rip." I told her Bella's story and showed her the stack of printouts.

Katie paged through them. "I've heard about this stuff. A bunch of pre-workout powders have similar ingredients. One nearly ended the career of a star athlete. He tested positive for amphetamine use and they weren't going to let him compete. He swore up and down he'd never touched the stuff. His coach backed him up and said something must be giving a false positive result."

"A likely story."

"No, some foods will do that. If you eat a poppy seed bagel a day or two before a drug test, you might test positive for morphine or codeine. They did an investigation into everything the star ate and drank. Turned out he was using one of these weight-loss powders to boost his performance and that's why he tested positive for amphetamines. He had no idea. The label said it was full of caffeine, but never mentioned the other stuff. That shit is addictive and similar to meth."

"What would it do to Juliet? Lydia Du Pres told her to take six scoops a day."

Katie frowned. "Are you sure she said that? Two scoops are about seven and a half grams. That's more than enough for a muscle-bound man. Six could seriously sicken a slim girl like Juliet, maybe even kill her. At the very least, she could become addicted. Why was Lydia Du Pres pushing this junk on Juliet?"

"Because she wanted her own daughter, Bella, to be DV Queen. She was jealous of Juliet's beauty and told her she had a fat rear end."

"You're shitting me. Lydia's ass is six ax handles wide. Juliet actually believed that malicious old bat?"

"Juliet was sixteen and trusting. Lydia was her aunt and her best friend's mother. I don't think Juliet had the kind of mind that would understand someone as devious as Lydia. You know how body conscious teen girls are. Juliet was beautiful, but she had a young girl's insecurity. Lydia used the ultimate F-word – fat – and Juliet was in tears. Bella said Juliet starting crying so hard, Lydia had trouble calming her down until she said she had the solution to Juliet's so-called problem – the Rad Rip weight loss powder."

Katie looked furious. "What a fucking waste. She wanted to kill that beautiful girl so her homely daughter could be a DV Queen."

"I wouldn't call Bella homely," I said, "but she's not in Juliet's league. She's the kind of girl who's good at field hockey and soccer. Lydia wanted a blonde princess who'd look pretty in white satin and heels."

"I'm not from here, Angela, but I don't get this DV Ball shit," Katie said. "I've never been to one – and I probably never will. But Evarts goes. He tells me a fat old rich guy dresses up like an Arabian king and then the Queen and the Maids bow down to him. I know the Forest lives in the past, but rich young women aren't presented to society and auctioned off to the highest bidder any more. Is that shit taken seriously in this day and age?"

"It is. By some of the parents," I said. "Most of the girls hate the whole deb scene, but their parents make them do it. The daughters are the pawns in this 'mine's bigger' game. The DV Ball would be laughable if the poor girls weren't so miserable."

"And you actually think Lydia would kill Juliet so her daughter could be Queen of the DV Ball. That's a little extreme."

"Remember the Texas mother who got nabbed for trying to hire a hit man to kill her daughter's rival? That was for a *junior high* cheerleading contest. The way Bella's mother sees it, spending another twenty thou so her daughter will be set for life is an investment in her future. What's a little murder when Lydia's already spending gobs of money and donating her own time at the Savant Shop? You ask me, Lydia killed Juliet."

Katie leaned back in her chair. "Whoa, that's serious shit. I won't have the tox screen back until tomorrow. Jace told me the victim's prints and an unknown person's prints were found on that bag with the unknown substance."

"It's not an unknown powder. It's Rad Rip, Katie. And those are Lydia's prints. I know it."

"You know it, but I need to prove it. We need to know whose prints are on that bag."

"What about the water bottle?"

"Just Juliet's prints, and it contained vodka, not water."

"Could Jace get a warrant to search Bella's house for the Rad Rip and also get her mother's prints?"

Katie laughed. "Not a chance. What judge – much less a Forest judge – would give a cop a warrant based on an unsigned text and your speculation?"

"The text is from Lydia's daughter."

"But the judge won't know that. You're using Bella to implicate her mother in a murder. Doesn't that bother you?"

"Not really. It's the only way to find out who killed Juliet. Besides, I'm helping Bella."

"How? I wanna hear this." Katie folded her arms and waited for my explanation.

"Bella's being blackmailed to go along with her mother's DV Queen plan. Lydia took away the girl's car until the committee okays Bella for Queen. She's trapped and I'm helping her out of it."

"That poor deprived child." Katie's sarcasm was thick as maple syrup. "Did it ever occur to you that Bella could live without having her own car? If she sucked it up and grew a backbone, she wouldn't have to be Queen. She could even get a part-time job flipping burgers and buy her own wheels."

"Her parents would never let her work with the Toonerville peasants. When this story gets out, that's the end of any chance Bella will have to be DV Queen. She'll be free. And Lydia will be drummed out of the Chouteau Forest Women's Club."

"Uneasy lies the head that wears a crown," Katie said.

"Exactly. But I know how to get Lydia's fingerprints."

Katie sighed. "If you do anything illegal and lose your job, I'll kick your ass from one end of Gravois to the other."

"What I'm going to do is perfectly legal."

"Would Jace do it?"

"No. It's not legal for him, but it is for me."

"Don't talk in riddles, Angela."

"I know how to get Lydia's prints legally," I said. "It would save Jace time and trouble."

"Okay, just watch yourself." She looked at her watch. "I have to go check on that poor girl again, and I don't have much patience."

"When can you autopsy her?"

"Tomorrow morning, I hope."

"By the time you have the results, I'll have her killer's prints. And I won't break a single law."

CHAPTER 17

Thursday, December 29, 7:30 p.m.
& Friday morning, December 30

Jace stopped me in the SOS parking lot as I was heading for my car.

"Do you know where Katie is? She's not in her office."

"It's time for the next two-hour check on Juliet," I said.

"She's still doing that?"

"The poor girl's still frozen. Katie's been sleeping in the SOS doctors lounge and living at the office since they brought her in."

"I'll say one thing, Katie's dedicated."

Katie wasn't the only one. I noticed how tired the big detective looked. His sad eyes were sunk into dark baggy bruises, and he needed a shave. This case was taking its toll on him.

"When is Katie doing the autopsy?"

"Tomorrow morning, I think. I have something that could be a lead."

"Let's talk about it in the cafeteria over bad coffee," he said.

"Too sensitive." I checked to make sure no one was within earshot. Way across the lot, I saw a nurse helping a shaky older woman into a wheelchair, while a gray-haired man tried to help. Otherwise, the lot was deserted.

"What the hell, Angela. Is the CIA following you or what?"

"I'm being extra cautious because I think one of the Forest's big guns killed Juliet." I lowered my voice. "Lydia Du Pres."

"Bella's mother?"

"Yeah. Bella told me something weird happened at the party. Her mother gave Juliet a weight loss powder."

"Girls always take that stuff."

"But this is different. Rad Rip is laced with amphetamines. Lydia told the girl she was fat."

Jace's eyes widened. "Juliet? That skinny little girl? Lydia called her fat?"

"The biggest F-word." I spilled the story of how Lydia had tormented Juliet and told her to take six times the normal dose to lose fat she didn't have, while Jace said, "She did?" and "You're joking" and "I don't believe it."

"Believe it," I finished. "She killed that poor girl so her own daughter could be DV Queen. That's why Lydia wouldn't let you talk to Bella. The kid has the key to Juliet's murder."

"Wait a minute," Jace said. "Did Lydia know her daughter was watching when she gave that girl a dangerous powder?"

"I don't think so." Actually, I didn't know. I'd never bothered to ask.

"How does Bella fit in? Was she really Juliet's friend, or was she jealous?" Jace asked. "Maybe she's the one who wanted to be Queen."

"No way. She was crying when she told me now that Juliet's dead, her parents are forcing her to be a DV Queen. She didn't even want to be a Maid."

"I thought girls like to dress up and stuff."

"They do, but the smart ones think the DV Ball is ridiculous and outdated. Something from another century. Lydia's hell-bent on her daughter being Queen. She's convinced that Bella will meet Mr. Right and her future will be set."

"Doesn't Lydia want her daughter to go to college? Have a career?" Jace was scratching his head. "Excuse all the questions, but I'm not from here. Sometimes, I don't get this place."

I laughed. "You're not alone. Of course Bella will go to college. Probably the Vernet Academy and get a degree in advanced tea pouring and flower arranging."

"That doesn't sound very challenging."

"It isn't. In the old days, people used to say girls went to Vernet to get their MRS, and well-bred Forest girls are still expected to marry well. To someone like Lydia, who doesn't work outside the home, a rich marriage is more important than a career. The DV Ball was how Lydia snagged a Du Pres. She wants the same life for her daughter, never mind what Bella wants.

"It costs money to be a Maid at the DV Ball, and being Queen is even more expensive and time-consuming. Lydia talked Curtiss into giving the committee an extra twenty thou so their girl would be in the running for Queen."

Jace whistled. "I could send my kid to college for that."

"Bella rebelled and her mother cracked down on her. She took away Bella's wheels. That's a major punishment for a Forest kid. She won't get her car back unless she's nice to the old trouts on the DV Selection Committee. Lydia also bribed Bella with a new phone to play along."

"It's that important?"

"Her daughter's future is a matter of life and death. Lydia almost got away with murder. She gave that Rad Rip to her daughter's rival. It's murder, Jace, and it's quick and clean. No messy stabbing, no bloody shooting. Nothing to clean up. No body to hide.

"At the party, Lydia gave a drunk teenager a big bag of amphetamine-laced powder. The kid takes some Rad Rip at the party. Now she's drunk *and* high. On the ride home, Juliet had a fight with her boyfriend, jumped out of his car and ran into the woods where she froze to death. Officially, her death is a tragic accident. There's no way to connect it to Lydia.

"Better yet, if Juliet survived the trip home, she had a big bag of amphetamine powder – enough to kill herself five or six times."

I stood there, waiting for Jace to pat me on the back. I'd solved the case. I was disappointed by his answer.

"Whoa, there, Angela, you've convicted Lydia before Katie's even autopsied the girl. All we have is Bella's word that her mother gave Juliet that bag of powder – the word of a teen who's pissed at her mother. We can't trust what Bella says."

"We don't have to. We have the evidence. The tech found the humongous bag at the scene with Juliet's clothes. The lab says there are unknown fingerprints on the bag. Those prints belong to Lydia."

"You *think* the prints belong to Lydia. We can't do anything until after the autopsy is done and the tox screens are back. *If* we have evidence that Juliet died of an amphetamine overdose, then I can investigate your claim. Right now, no judge is going to give me a search warrant or let me take Lydia's prints."

"That's what Katie said." I had a hard time hiding my disappointment.

"I don't want to pour cold water over your theory." I winced at Jace's poor choice of words. "We don't know what killed Juliet. She could have died of exposure. Or alcohol poisoning. She could have been attacked by someone in the woods. Or fell on those rocks by the creek and broken her neck. We can't go attacking anyone, much less a Forest bigwig, without proof."

Jace could see my disappointment. He tried to make me feel better. "Thanks for choosing the right place to discuss a touchy subject. It wouldn't have been good for either of us if we'd been overheard."

I mustered a smile and told the overworked detective good night. As I drove home, I decided that nothing he'd said had changed my mind. I would get Lydia's fingerprints, and I wouldn't use Bella. Katie was right; I couldn't ask the girl to incriminate her own mother.

Besides, Lydia was shrewd – look how she'd set up that elaborate plan to kill Juliet. If she thought someone suspected her, she'd throw away the Rad Rip powder. Then it would be even harder to prove her role in Juliet's death.

I knew exactly how I'd get those fingerprints. Back at home, I called the Savant Shop. A recording said the shop was closed and the hours were ten a.m. to five p.m. Tuesday through Saturday.

The Savant Shop was on Gravois Road in the tony Forest shopping district that was all dark green awnings and fresh white paint. The next morning, I was there at five minutes past ten o'clock. The shop had a wreath on the door, as required by Forest law, with a preppie plaid bow so the old guard knew it was a safe place.

The brass bell over the door tinkled when I entered. To my left were racks of vintage ball gowns and cocktail dresses, festooned with black lace, bows, and beads. To my right were shelves of dusty crystal, tarnished silver candlesticks and gewgaws, and second-line appliances that looked like unwanted wedding gifts.

Straight ahead behind the counter was a woman who could be Bella Du Pres thirty pounds and thirty years into the future. Her name tag read "Lydia." Our ancestors made women with Lydia's big breasts and wide hips into fertility goddesses, but she was born in the wrong era.

"May I help you?" Lydia forced a smile.

"Just looking." I saw the woman's shoulders slump and boredom reclaim her features. She went back to reading a glossy *Forest Society* magazine.

I roamed the shelves, looking for something that would show Lydia's fingerprints. The knickknacks needed serious cleaning. I was glad I'd slipped a damp cloth into a Ziploc bag and stuck it in my purse. I skipped the silver. I was surprised the shop was selling a tarnish-blackened silent butler. I hadn't seen one since my mother had worked for Old Reggie. Back when people smoked like chimneys, hostesses had these fancy long-handled metal contraptions about the size of cigar boxes. The contents of overflowing ashtrays were dumped into the silent butlers and whisked away.

I tried to find an overpriced ornament I could afford. Seventy-five dollars for a chipped Waterford vase? No way. Besides, I was pretty sure cut glass wouldn't show fingerprints. Ditto for the forty-five-dollar cut glass candy dish missing its lid. I searched for smooth glass objects. Twenty bucks seemed awfully pricey for a clunky glass ashtray, but maybe I could use it for burglar protection. Bean intruders with it.

I bypassed the simpering glass angel with the lumpy wings – not a good surface anywhere. The tea light holders were equally dubious.

At last I saw it. A smooth, bulbous glass vase, the kind florists gave away free with flower arrangements. It was perfectly plain, and marked SALE. Ten bucks for a free vase – and that was five dollars off the original price.

There's something I can afford, I thought. I held it up to the light. The vase had more fingerprints than a police lab.

I heard Lydia clear her throat. "Are you sure I can't help you?" This time, Bella's mother sounded more forceful. I realized I must look suspicious—the vase could fit into my big black purse.

"Just checking this vase for chips or flaws."

I was grateful when the doorbell tinkled genteelly. Maybe the glass angel had sent this distraction. An older woman with spun-silver hair entered the shop. "Lydia, darling, I'm so glad you're here. You must help me find a cocktail dress. Something in black, please."

"You've come to the right place, Mrs. Du Champ," Lydia said.

Boy, have you, I thought. And at the right time, too.

"We have a lovely little Valentino in your size, if you like velvet, and I can show you a sweet little Chanel."

The two women discussed the merits of various dresses while I stuffed my gloves in my pocket and wiped the vase with the damp cloth, then polished it with my wool scarf. When Lydia escorted her customer to the dressing room and left her with several dresses, I put my gloves back on and carried the newly polished vase to the counter.

"I'll take this," I said.

"May I wrap it for you?"

"Please."

Lydia carefully wrapped the vase in white tissue paper, leaving her fingerprints all over the smooth glass. "You can do so much with these simple vases, can't you?"

"I hope so," I said.

CHAPTER 18

Friday, December 30, 10:43 a.m.

I left the Savant Shop with my prize: the glass vase plastered with the killer's prints. After stashing it safely in my car trunk, I drove home. I was on call today at the ME's office and prayed that nobody else would die. Two deaths were already too much tragedy.

Katie was autopsying Juliet this morning. I paced my kitchen restlessly, poured another cup of coffee to amp up the caffeine jitters, and waited for word. Most autopsies took two to four hours, but there was nothing routine about Juliet's death. How long would Katie take to post the girl? How quickly would she get back the tox tests? Those could take four to six weeks, but Juliet's family had clout and cash. Maybe Katie would get the answers quicker.

I glanced at the clock: 11:47. I climbed the stairs and made my bed, then cleaned the upstairs bathroom. And checked the clock. Again.

It was 12:11. The clock's hands crawled forward like they'd been stomped.

My cell chimed and I pounced on it, wondering what grisly news was waiting for me. Did Katie know what killed Juliet? Or would I have to investigate another death? More holiday sorrow?

I nearly laughed with relief. The text was from Daisy. I owed her and Bella a ride to the Olive Garden for delivering on her promise.

Can you take me and Bella to the mall? Daisy texted.

No Olive Garden? I texted back.

Daisy texted, *Better than the OG! Brock wants to take Bella out New Year's Eve!!! That's like tomorrow! Needs to look extra hot!!! I need one, too. I'm going out with Rush.*

Be there in ten, I answered.

I heard the steady plop, plop of snow melting on my roof. My Charger was frosted with road salt. The Forest's icing-white post-Christmas snow was now dirty gray sludge.

Traffic was light. I saw the ribboned wreath on Daisy's front door fluttering in the warm breeze, and the two girls tumbled outside, dressed in light jackets, hair shining, eyes bright. Juliet might be on a morgue table now, but her friends seemed lighthearted, giggly, and very young. Their mourning was over before Juliet's funeral.

In the car, Daisy took the obligatory selfie without any drama and sent it to her mother. The usually blasé girls eagerly discussed their plans for New Year's Eve.

"I can't believe Brock called me," Bella said. "For like no reason."

"There's a reason," Daisy said. "He wants to say goodbye."

Brock? I thought. The guy who had a fight with Juliet at Bella's fatal party.

"Where's Brock going?" I asked.

"He's leaving the country," Bella said. "His parents are sending him to Switzerland at the start of the new semester. He's leaving New Year's Day."

"He'll be flying to Europe hungover." Daisy giggled.

"That's why I need a hot dress for New Year's Eve," Bella said. "He won't be back until next summer."

Despite her tough talk about hook ups, Bella had a crush on Brock. The boy's sudden uprooting made me suspicious. Forest creatures were not jet setters. "Why is he leaving in the middle of the school year?" I asked.

"He's wanted to go away to Switzerland like forever," Bella said. "He's a good skier."

"He was at your party, right?" I asked. Didn't he call Juliet a slut for dating Dex and slam his fist into a wall? Remember Juliet, the good friend you said you'll never forget? This morning, she had her head buzzed open with a Stryker saw. Her pretty face was peeled back like a rubber mask. I fought to control my disgust at their heartless lack of concern. I needed my questions answered.

"Brock is smokin'," Bella said. "I can't believe he wants to go out with me."

That's because the girl he really wants is dead, Bella. After Juliet fought with Dex and charged out of his car into the woods, did your favorite hottie attack her, tear off her clothes, then leave her to freeze to death?

I was screaming those words in my head, but Daisy and Bella were oblivious. I asked, "When did Brock leave your party, Bella?"

"Right after Juliet and Dex. I was afraid that would break it up, but everyone else stayed until after five."

"Those three missed the best breakfast," Bella said. "I love bacon and eggs after partying all night."

Never mind that Juliet was probably dead by then. "What kind of car does Brock drive?"

"A really sweet Beemer." I glanced in the rearview mirror and saw a starry-eyed Bella. "He drives a black Z4, the two-seater convertible. He got it for his sixteenth birthday."

"Amazing," I said. It was. What kind of parents bought a sixteen-year-old a $50,000 convertible? The kind who shipped him off to school in Switzerland when things turned rocky.

"I'll send you a photo," Bella said. "He gave me a ride when he got it in September."

"He gave everyone a ride." Daisy couldn't resist bringing her friend down a notch.

"Why do his parents want to get Brock out of the country because he was at your party?" I asked.

Bella shrugged. "Nothing happened. We had a good time. His parents want him to go into politics and if Juliet was murdered and he had to testify it could be bad for his future."

"Like that Kennedy boy," Daisy added. "People thought he killed that girl just because he was at a party years ago and she died afterward. I'm not sure if he did it or not."

"Doesn't make any difference." Bella nodded her head wisely. "It hurt him. Brock can't take that risk."

Brock had been at a party with illicit drugs, underage drinking, and a teenage girl who disappeared on her way home and was found naked and frozen two days later. Word would come out that Brock was jealous and had slammed his fist in the wall.

I had to get this news to Jace right after I dropped the girls at the mall. I was caught in traffic on Gravois Road now, slowly rolling through the chichi Forest shopping district. "Do you want to shop here before we go to the mall?"

"Boring." Bella dragged the word out until it was at least three syllables.

"Remember that dress my mom brought home from the Savant Shop?" Daisy asked. "She wanted me to wear it to the Holly Dance."

"As if." Bella sneered. "It was pink chiffon. Like a freaking Disney princess."

"With a humongous pink bow on my boobs," Daisy said.

I steered the Charger onto the highway. From the back seat, Daisy's voice turned into a parody of what was probably her mother. "Now, Daisy, you must dress like a lady. This dress is sweet and elegant. Show a man too much and he loses interest."

The girls dissolved into mocking cackles. I was relieved when I turned off the highway exit to the West Forest Mall. I threaded through the traffic. "Which entrance, ladies?"

"The one by Forever 21," Daisy said.

I dropped them at the entrance. "We'll text you when we're finished," Daisy said.

"I could be on a case, ladies. I'm on call today."

"Then we'll walk over to the Olive Garden and wait. Bye." Dismissed.

I waited until the mall entrance swallowed the girls, then parked and checked my phone for Bella's photo of Brock's black two-seater Beemer. The boy was fondling its curved backside as if he wanted to be alone with it in a dark garage. Bella, draped on the shining hood, was showing acres of leg and cleavage, smiling an invitation Brock didn't notice.

Brock's charm escaped me. He looked thick-necked and thick-headed, with short blond hair and a self-satisfied sneer. If Bella caught this future politico, she'd play second fiddle to his massive ego. His wife was doomed to have two blond children, a golden retriever, and an adoring smile.

I called Jace. He sounded more chipper today. "I've got more news for you," I said.

"Angela, do we have the autopsy results yet?" Was he suppressing a sigh?

I rushed forward. "Not yet, but Katie should call any time. Meanwhile, a kid who was at Bella's holiday party is suddenly leaving."

"She's going out of town?"

"*He's* leaving the country. The runner is Brock Sedgwick, the kid who punched his fist through a wall. When Juliet was found, his parents decided he should go to school in Switzerland. He leaves New Year's Day."

"Interesting. Why the big move?"

"Daisy and Bella say Brock likes to ski."

"They could send him to Vail."

"The girls also say his parents don't want a future President connected with a possible murder investigation."

"That sounds more like it. I'll have to move carefully, but I'll make sure everything is in place once Katie gives us the answers later today. Getting his passport flagged so he can't leave the country should be a couple of phone calls. I may have to get a court order or get the feds involved.

"I'll definitely need a search warrant for his body so we can get a DNA swab and document the injury on his hand. I'll start drafting it. That has to be done quick. Wounds heal and the evidence could vanish. I might also find his DNA in or on the broken drywall in Bella's house."

"Can't you serve it now?"

"Not until after the autopsy. You know that."

"I hope the Du Presses haven't patched that hole yet," I said. "I'm sending you a photo of Brock's car with Bella perched on the hood. The license plate is visible."

"Thanks. I could get the license, but this will save time. I've already requested the security footage from all the estates from Bella's home to Juliet's house, so we can see if the kid followed her and Dex. I'll need video backup with the kind of lawyers these parents can afford. I'd better get cracking."

My cell chimed right after he hung up. Bella texted me, *We scored big time. Meet us by Nordstrom.*

The two girls were at the entrance, holding their dress bags. "You won't believe what we got," Bella said.

"On sale, too," Daisy said.

On the trip home, I listened to them debate the merits of ombre sequins, fringe, keyhole cutouts and lace inserts. They would have sounded girlishly charming if their friend wasn't lying dead in the morgue.

As I pulled into Daisy's drive, my cell chimed again. I braked and checked the text. Katie! It said, *Meet me at my office ASAP. Jace is on the way.*

At last. The girls hurried out of the car, still talking about their dresses. "I wish I'd had time for a custom fitting." Bella slammed the door without a thank you.

I didn't notice. I roared off to hear about the girl with the very latest custom work: a Y-incision stitched on her silken white chest.

CHAPTER 19

Friday, December 30, 3:52 p.m.

Jace and I pelted Katie with questions in her shoe box office. The room could barely hold the three of us.

"Hold it!" Katie said. "I can't breathe with you two in here, hurling questions. I'm at the end of my rope. I've been living at SOS for two days, watching over a dead girl. I'm sleep deprived. The whole Forest will be after my head when the results are released. Evarts says he'll back me, but he conveniently skipped town for a three-day visit to Kansas City."

"Kansas in the winter," I said. "Who wouldn't jump at the chance?"

"Quiet," Katie said.

I regretted my stupid comment. Katie looked ragged. Her skin was oily, her eyes peered out from bruise-like half-circles, her lab coat was clean but wrinkled, and her brown hair needed a wash.

"I'm on my own when the shit storm hits, and it will have mostly blown over by the time His Majesty returns on Monday, ready to smile for the TV cameras. Now, if you want to hear my conclusion, keep quiet. Jace, sit in my chair." Katie pushed her desk chair toward the detective.

"I can stand."

"You can, but you look worse than I do. I can't talk if I'm worrying you'll fall face forward onto my desk. Sit. And you, Angela, sit down and light somewhere. Your flittering is driving me nuts."

I perched on the edge of the desk. Katie stood behind it, the skull with the plastic poinsettia grinning at us through the fake foliage. Jace was crammed into the chair, barely able to move.

"Now, to answer your questions. Yes, I have the tox screens and the blood work."

"That was fast," Jace said.

Katie glared him back into silence.

"Normally, we have a backlog of a couple of weeks, but this isn't a normal case. I was mainly looking for drugs and alcohol, and those results are quicker. Doc Bartlett can get lab results in a day or two. Juliet's family is rich and connected. They demanded – and got – extra fast results. We contract out our lab services and Juliet's were fast-tracked to the head of the line."

I tried not to fidget. Tell us something we don't know, I thought.

"Let me tell you what the tests showed. First, Juliet wasn't raped. There was no seminal fluid on her or in her."

"That will be a relief for her family," Jace said.

I felt relieved, too. I'd never spoken or even seen the girl when she was alive, but a death investigation creates a curious intimacy. I was glad Juliet was spared that ordeal.

"Was she sexually active?" I asked.

"Yes, but it appears the sex was consensual and there's no way to tell who her partner was."

"No rape means both boys are off the hook," Jace said. "Juliet's parents will be furious. They're convinced Dex killed her. They've pulled every string they can to get me to arrest the kid when he's in the hospital."

"Is he still in a coma?" I asked.

"He's coming around," Jace said. "He'll be hurting for a while, with head injuries and a broken arm, but he should be okay."

"Glad to hear it," Katie said. "The LaRouches are so hot for his hide, they even called Evarts and tried to get him to use his influence to arrest Dex. That's another reason he headed for Kansas.

"Let's continue. Juliet was drinking beer and vodka. I could smell it when I opened her up. Her BAC – blood alcohol count – was .30. She was drinking up until the time she died. You found the water bottle with the vodka."

Jace raised his eyebrows. "That's way over the legal limit. It's .08 for grownups. For anyone under twenty-one, .02 is legally drunk."

"Isn't that for driving – DUIs?" I asked.

"Thank God she wasn't driving," Katie said. "She shouldn't have been walking around. She got shit-faced at a party where adults were serving alcohol to minors."

Jace started to make a sound and Katie cut him off.

"I know, there's nothing you can do about it, Jace. All the Forest bigwigs use the same excuse: 'It's better if the kids learn to drink in the safety of their home,' but there is no supervision. The parents go to their rooms and the kids guzzle everything they get their hands on. I hope the LaRouches sue the socks off Bella's parents. That's the only way to stop parents from serving alcohol to minors.

"Usually kids that drunk barf their guts out and fall asleep," Katie said. "Juliet was hammered enough to get fighting mad, and picked a fight with her boyfriend."

"So she fought with Dex on the way home and ran off into the woods in below-zero weather, wearing practically nothing," I said.

"Yep. Her coordination, balance and vision were off, and her reaction times were slow. She was damn unlucky. Most kids that drunk fall asleep. If she'd ralphed and then passed out, she'd still be alive today."

"What about amphetamines?" I asked.

"The lab said the bag of white powder contained an 'amphetamine-like substance' but there was no trace of amphetamines in her blood."

"Then Lydia's off the hook," I said. "I got her fingerprints for nothing."

"You got them?" Jace said. "How?"

"I wasted ten dollars buying a plain glass vase from the Savant Shop, where she volunteers. I cleaned it first and then she wrapped it for me in tissue paper. Her prints are all over it."

"Let me print that vase," Jace said. "I may be able to use that information if Bella Du Pres's family gives me any trouble."

"I didn't hear that," Katie said. "Do you want to know what killed Juliet?"

Jace and I nodded.

"She did not have a broken neck, or head wounds. She wasn't poisoned or strangled. There were no broken bones, just a few minor scrapes, cuts and bruises from falling. She didn't have a stroke or any detectable disease. From what I can determine, she was a perfectly healthy sixteen-year-old."

So what killed Juliet LaRouche?

The unspoken question hovered in the air. We waited for Katie to answer it, too afraid to say something.

The skull with the plastic poinsettia grinned at us. I watched a sweat drop roll down Jace's forehead. The room was hot and claustrophobic. I wanted to unbutton my coat, but was afraid to move.

We were so quiet, I heard the cheap clock mark another sixty seconds. We were now one minute closer to our own deaths.

At last, Katie spoke. "Juliet's death was a rare case of paradoxical undressing."

"What?" Jace said.

"That's where a person who's freezing to death undresses while she's dying from the cold," I said. "I read about that. A person's thermostat goes haywire and while the temperature may be below zero, they feel overheated and throw off their clothes. I thought that happened mostly to older people."

"It does," Katie said. "But young, healthy adults can also be victims, especially if they've been drinking. And the flower of the Forest aristocracy was drunk as a skunk."

"I'll be damned," Jace said. "Her parents are never going to accept that. And I'm going to have to tell them."

"I'll go with you," I said.

"That's not your job."

"Yes it is," I said. "And you'll need a witness."

CHAPTER 20

Friday, December 30, 6:15 p.m.

"What killed my daughter?" Prentice LaRouche asked. "I have to know. He has to pay for this … this despicable crime."

I could hardly believe the skeleton sitting across from us was the same vigorous man who'd pounded on my front door three days ago. Jace and I sat on a pale brocade sofa. Juliet's parents were in adjoining wing chairs by the marble fireplace.

"Thank gawd Missouri has the death penalty," Prentice said. "He did it, didn't he?"

Prentice LaRouche's hand shook as he picked up a crystal glass of scotch from the table next to his chair. He seemed unable to say Dexter's name. Dread seized me. This was going to be even worse than I expected.

A hollow-eyed Midge twisted a lace handkerchief. Her eyes were red and swollen, but she didn't cry. I wondered if she had any tears left. Midge's dirty hair needed a stylist's attention. Her face had collapsed into wrinkles. She wore no makeup and a shapeless black dress. On the table by her chair a gold-rimmed tea cup sat untouched.

From its place over the marble mantelpiece, Midge's debutante portrait smiled down. The radiant young woman in the gold-framed painting looked like a distant, luckier cousin of the raddled, broken woman in the living room.

The fireplace was cold, and the photos of the luminous Juliet on the piano and the table tops were draped in black ribbon. The room smelled like a florist's shop. Bouquets and plants bristling with sympathy cards crowded every surface.

I braced myself. I knew Jace's news would bring the LaRouches fresh sorrow.

"There was no crime." Jace's voice was gentle. "Your daughter is dead, and that news is as bad as can be. But she wasn't, uh ... assaulted in any way."

Midge's agonized howls made the hair stand on the back of my neck.

Jace dutifully recited Katie's findings, delicately avoiding the word *autopsy*. "The medical examiner said Juliet wasn't injured in any way, she didn't have a stroke, she didn't break her neck, she ... "

Prentice slammed down his drink so hard it spilled on the table. "Don't tell me what didn't happen. Quit stalling! How was she murdered? I demand to know!"

"She wasn't murdered," Jace said.

"Impossible!"

"She died in a freak accident, sir."

"Without her clothing? That's absurd!"

"It happens, sir. Her death was a rare case of something called paradoxical undressing. The temperature was below zero and she was freezing to death, but her body went haywire and she felt hot and threw off all her clothes. To her, it felt like a summer's day, and she was overheated."

"I've never heard of such of a thing!" Prentice glared at Jace. "My daughter would never take off all her clothes, not even on the hottest days of summer."

"Paradoxical undressing is very rare, but it happens."

Prentice stalked over to the flower-packed sideboard and poured himself another drink.

In the awkward silence, Midge managed a hesitant sentence. Her shoulders were hunched as if she expected to be beaten. "Juliet was only a short distance from her home. I don't understand how she could freeze to death within sight of her house. She was perfectly healthy."

"Yes, ma'am, but she was extremely intoxicated."

"That can't be true!" Prentice was shouting now. He pounded the top of the sideboard. "My daughter didn't drink! She was sixteen! She was at a chaperoned party given by one of the first families. By her aunt and uncle!"

"Mr. and Mrs. Du Pres went upstairs to their room and let the kids have a good time," Jace said. "I'm sorry to say that included underage drinking. The medical examiner said Juliet had a blood alcohol level of .30. She'd been drinking beer and vodka."

"He gave it to her! He forced her to drink it." Prentice still wouldn't say Dex's name. He paced the room, unable to master his fury.

"No one forced your daughter to drink anything," Jace said. "Her water bottle was found with her. It contained a few ounces of vodka and only her fingerprints were on that bottle. Witnesses said she played beer pong and drank beer, then later switched to Grey Goose vodka."

Witnesses who talked to me, but wouldn't talk to the police, I thought.

"No!" Midge's voice was a squeak, not a scream.

Jace and I stayed silent and waited for the terrible news to sink in. Juliet's parents had grown up in the Forest. They'd drunk alcohol at parties when they were teenagers. They also knew when those privileged teens drove home drunk, the officers let them off with a warning – if they even stopped them. Why wasn't this police officer cooperating like the others?

"You have to arrest that boy!" Prentice shouted, but this time, his voice lacked authority.

"He's done nothing wrong, sir. There is no evidence of murder."

"Who performed this travesty of an examination on my daughter?"

"Dr. Katie Kelly Stern, the assistant medical examiner. Dr. Evarts Evans agreed with her conclusions."

Prentice glared at me, acknowledging me for the first time. "Young lady, you work for the medical examiner. Is that true?"

"Yes, Mr. LaRouche. Dr. Evans is out of town until Monday, but he agreed with Dr. Stern's report."

"Then I'll talk to him when he returns."

"Mr. LaRouche, there's one other thing you should know," Jace said. "A Ziploc bag of white powder was found with Juliet's clothes. It was analyzed and found to contain an amphetamine-like substance. A witness said Lydia Du Pres gave that bag of powder to your daughter. It's very addictive."

Jace was really laying it on, I thought. He must want to punish Bella's mother for trying to kill Juliet.

"Why would Lydia give our daughter amphetamines?" Midge sounded dazed.

"The witness said Lydia told Juliet that she was fat."

"My Juliet? Fat? Why that old witch. She's big as a house. How dare she." Midge's anger put color in her cheeks again and she showed a flash of her old spirit.

Jace continued his destruction of Lydia. "Juliet was very upset by her comments. Lydia told your daughter if she took this substance – it's a weight-loss powder called Rad Rip – she would lose the extra fat."

"But Juliet wasn't fat!"

"I know, Mrs. LaRouche. As I understand it, Lydia was jealous of your daughter's beauty. She wanted her own daughter to be DV Queen."

"Outrageous!" Prentice said. "There's no way Bella will ever attend the DV Ball again. I'm calling my attorney immediately. I'm suing Bella Du Pres's family. And that boy's family. I'll shut down that car shop. It's an eyesore. I'll ruin the lot of them, the way they've ruined my daughter.

"You may go now. Both of you." Prentice marched out of the room without looking back.

Midge managed a tentative smile and tried to excuse her husband's rude behavior. "Juliet was daddy's little girl. This is hard on him. Is there anything else?"

"No, Mrs. LaRouche."

"Could I ask you a question? Did she suffer?"

"Not at all. She was feeling no pain," I said.

Midge heard the conviction in my voice and sighed. "Thank you. That's a relief. I couldn't bear the thought that my little girl died alone and in pain."

Midge escorted us to the front door. "Thank you for coming to tell us in person. Prentice is upset now. The news is so shocking. He needs to get used to the idea, but he'll come around."

I felt a stab of pity for Juliet's mother. "I'm so sorry for your loss, Mrs. LaRouche."

"I know you are, dear."

As Midge quietly closed the massive front door, the black mourning wreath rattled against the cold wood. The night was dark and moonless, and the temperature had dropped. I pulled my coat tighter and wished I'd brought my scarf to protect me from the freezing wind. Dead leaves scuttled across the courtyard and heavy grim clouds promised more snow. The sky was drained of light and life.

Inside Jace's car, the detective soon had the heater blasting warm air, but I couldn't stop shivering. We sat in the courtyard a moment to recover from the wrenching scene.

"You did a good job, Jace." I smiled at him. "You really went after Lydia."

"She deserved it," Jace said. "That woman tried to murder Juliet, and there's no way I could prove it."

"You're catching on how the locals operate," I said. "The Forest will punish her, and they'll show no mercy."

"Juliet's father didn't accept Katie's conclusions," Jace said. "Can he make trouble for her?"

"He can try, but Evarts signed off on it, too, and he'll prevail," I said. "Prentice will raise hell for a while, and then he'll start suing. Prentice wants to crush Dex's family. He'll sue them for impeding an investigation and lying to the police because the Gordons ordered Dex to go to his grandparents' house. Prentice will try to nail them for obstruction of justice and false information. He'll claim if the Gordons had told him where Juliet was when he pounded on their door, his daughter would be alive."

"He'll have a hard time getting what he wants," Jace said. "Katie can testify that Juliet was already dead by the time Prentice banged on Dex's door. No charges will be filed against the boy or his family. Prentice will have to bring civil suits and most of the jury will be from Toonerville – the rich are good at getting out of jury duty. Dex's family will have a real jury of their peers."

"Then Prentice will start suing Bella's family," I said. "He'll make someone pay for his daughter's death."

"Juliet's already paid," Jace said. "You ask me, her parents' snobbery killed her. If they'd let her date that Toonerville boy, it would have been one more teen romance. Those rarely last. Instead, they said no and made Dex and his car exotic and forbidden."

"Dex and Juliet would have broken up for good the night of Bella's party," I said, "and that would have been the end of the Toonerville boy.

"If Dex had been allowed to drive Juliet to her house, she would have been a beautiful Queen, instead of a beautiful corpse."

EPILOGUE

New Year's Day and beyond

Juliet was dazzling in death. Her white skin was flawless, her hair icy blonde, her pale lips slightly parted. When they finished preparing her, the morticians at the Chouteau Forest Funeral Home admired their handiwork as if they'd created her. Juliet lay in state in her snow white coffin, banked by white roses. The girl was designed to dazzle, and her unearthly beauty would be praised until the casket lid was closed.

I went to Juliet's wake and funeral. I felt a personal connection to the girl. My fruitless effort to save Juliet and my thankless investigation bound me to the victim in ways I couldn't explain. I hoped Juliet's parents wouldn't think I was one of the corpse flies, the older women who attended notable Forest deaths as if they were Broadway openings. Juliet's wake had attracted a bigger audience than usual. Even gawkers from Toonerville showed up.

Like nearly everyone, I wept when I saw Juliet.

At the funeral home, I stood for nearly an hour in the receiving line in the largest viewing room. I was behind Juliet's entire class at the

Chouteau Forest Academy. Bella and Daisy were in front of me, but the girls ignored me. I heard Bella whispering about her New Year's Eve date with Brock and how they'd hooked up in his pool house, and wished I couldn't hear the intimate details of their date.

I expected the students to erupt into nervous laughter or hijinks while waiting in the long line, but they were subdued. Many seemed to genuinely mourn their lost classmate. Juliet wore the black velvet strapless dress she'd worn to the Holly Ball, as if she'd be dancing forever. When Bella and Daisy knelt in front of the casket to pray for Juliet, I thought I heard Bella say, "Didn't Juliet wear that dress before?"

Fortunately, Juliet's parents didn't seem to hear that comment. Midge and Prentice seemed numb to the sympathy and murmured condolences. Hollowed out and old beyond their years, the LaRouches' reason for living was gone. Neither one appeared to recognize me when I finally reached them. Considering my connection with Juliet's death, perhaps it was just as well.

The day of Juliet's funeral was sweetly sunny and warm, a rare winter day that promised spring would come soon. I stayed at the back of the crowd, nearly hidden by gray granite tombstones. I was close enough to see Midge collapse when her daughter was lowered into the cold ground. Prentice's reaction looked different. He stiffened and his pale eyes seemed to burn with rage. I thought I had imagined that, until I heard what happened to Bella's family. Then I was sure Prentice had vowed to ruin the people who destroyed his daughter.

All the Forest's first families came to Juliet's wake and burial, except for Lydia Du Pres. The LaRouche family had a handwritten note delivered to Bella's mother, requesting her absence. Lydia didn't understand why a Du Pres would be barred from an important occasion. Perhaps they resented her because she had a living daughter who was going to be DV Queen. Lydia shrugged off the slight. Grief made people do strange things.

She volunteered to work at the Savant Shop on the day of Juliet's funeral, but her request was politely refused. She was shocked when she was asked not to return. No reason was given, but Lydia began to hear unpleasant whispers when she lunched at the Chouteau Forest Women's Club. Her favorite table was no longer available, and the service was slow. When she was in a stall in the ladies room, she heard one club woman say, "I can't believe Lydia has the nerve to show her face after what she did to poor little Juliet. Jealous old cow tried to poison that girl. Called her fat!"

"Just looking at her ruined my lunch," her companion said as she washed her hands and dried them on a monogrammed club towel. Between pumps on the china hand lotion bottle, Lydia heard these terrible words: "And talk about fat. Did you see the way she shoveled in the creamed chicken on toast – and asked for extra bread and butter?"

Their mocking laughter wounded Lydia so badly she waited until the ladies room was empty, then slipped out the service door and never returned. She resigned from the club the next day.

Bella passed the crucial interview, but was not chosen to be the Daughter of Versailles Queen. She wasn't even permitted to be a Maid. Her entire family was barred from ever attending a DV Ball again. Bella, who'd always hated the DV, felt oddly unhappy now that she couldn't attend.

Her father's "donation" to the Daughters of Versailles Committee was not refundable. The committee kept it.

Too bad. The family needed the money. After Juliet's funeral, her parents filed a substantial civil suit against Lydia and Curtiss Du Pres for serving liquor to their daughter. They settled out of court for an undisclosed amount. The LaRouche family used the money for a scholarship in Juliet's name.

Business suddenly dried up for Curtiss Du Pres, once a top earner at the Forest Mortgage Specialists. He lost his job and was forced to sell "starter homes" for a Toonerville real estate company. Thanks to Lydia's extensive sales experience at the Savant Shop, she was able to get a job at the Plus Size Warehouse in Toonerville, as well as a ten percent discount on their clothes. Bella's car was sold. On weekends and in the summer, she worked as a server at the Burger Den, and took the bus to work. Brock did not date her when he returned home from Switzerland that summer. In fact, he passed right by her, as if he didn't know her, but said loudly to a friend, "Do you smell fried onions?"

Brock's parents imported a handyman from St. Louis to fix the hole where Brock put his fist through the wall in the Du Pres's party room. They also paid for new wallpaper and rugs in the room. Bella's family signed an agreement that the incident would never be mentioned, effectively papering over that unpleasant incident. Once the repairs were made, the Du Pres family put their mansion up for sale and moved to a condo on the edge of Toonerville. Lydia told her co-workers that her life is much easier now that she doesn't have to worry about taking care of that big old house.

Dexter Gordon recovered from his injuries. His parents wisely decided the boy should not come back to the Forest. He moved in with his maternal grandparents in California and finished high school there. Attorney Montgomery Bryant filed a civil suit against the company that owned the West Forest Mall. My mall cop video convinced the mall to settle out of court for an undisclosed amount. Monty also sued the three people who attacked Dexter, and the boy was awarded more than two hundred thousand dollars for those assaults. Dex used the money to go to college in California and now works for a company designing what it calls "the cars of the future." His father's auto body shop continues to thrive. Prentice LaRouche's efforts to sue the family were unsuccessful.

I am superstitious about the first person to cross my threshold in the New Year. I believe that person sets the course for the rest of the year. I spent the first day of the New Year alone and on call, and I was relieved I wasn't needed to investigate any deaths. I wasn't needed on the second day, either. My shift ended at seven o'clock that night, and I built a roaring fire and settled in with a good book. I'd just gotten the fire blazing the way I liked when my doorbell rang. Katie was at my door with a box of dark chocolate, two wine bottles, and a big smile.

Once my friend stepped over my threshold, I was relieved. This would be a good year.

Katie looked fresh and rested. "Happy New Year!" she said, breezing into my living room. "The wine is for me, the sparkling grape juice is for you, and we're both going to eat the chocolate. Monty put his nephew on the plane home yesterday, making it truly a happy New Year for me."

"Judging by your glow," I said, "I suspect you had him all to yourself last night." Katie ignored me and said, "Where's my wine?"

I poured the drinks, and we toasted.

"To good times and a good year," I said. "And next year, we'll both toast with wine."

"I'll drink to that," Katie said.

And so we did.

ACKNOWLEDGMENTS

Ice Blonde kept me cool during a long, sweltering summer. I kept thinking back to those freezing Missouri winters. It's a peculiar humid cold that burrows into the bones, and though I live in Florida now, I've never forgotten it.

Writing a mystery is a group project, and I had a lot of help and advice for *Ice Blonde*.

First, thank you to my husband, Don Crinklaw, my first reader and true love, for your help and support, as well as the long discussions about life in Chouteau County. Don swears he went to college with some of its over-privileged inhabitants.

Thank you to my agent, Joshua Bilmes, president of JABberwocky Literary, for his help and guidance on this project, and his meticulous line editing of *Ice Blonde*. I also appreciate the efforts of the JABberwocky team, including Lisa Rodgers, literary agent and e-book manager, Patrick Disselhorst, ebook assistant, and the ever patient Susan Velazquez, agent's assistant. Tara O'Shea's ice-frosted cover gave me chills. Thanks to copyeditor Bryon Quertermous for some excellent catches.

I'm grateful to Bill Hopkins, retired Missouri judge and author of the Judge Rosswell Carew Mysteries, who helped with the legal details. Charles Hutchings, the Bollinger County, Missouri coroner, was on duty over the Christmas holidays to tell me how to defrost a frozen body. Detective R.C. White, Fort Lauderdale Police Department (retired) and licensed private eye, provided boundless help about police procedure.

Thank you to retired medicolegal death investigator Mary Fran Ernst, one of the authors of the training text, *Medicolegal Death Investigator*, and to death investigator Krysten Addison, as well as Harold R. Messler, retired manager-criminalistics, St. Louis Police Laboratory. Nurse and mystery writer Gregg Brickman helped with the medical information.

Many thanks to both Molly Portman and Alan Portman for their invaluable help on teen customs and tech info. Retired teacher Mary-Sue Carl of Bothell, Washington, also gave me a window into high school students' minds.

Special thanks to Will Graham, author of *Spider's Dance*. Joanna Campbell Slan, bestselling mystery author and Daphne du Maurier Award winner, along with Susan Schlueter of St. Louis, Jinny Gender of Kirkwood, Missouri, and Mary Alice Gorman and Richard Goldman of revuzeit.com also helped.

I cannot write without the help of many librarians, including Anne Watts, assistant library director of the Boynton Beach City Library, Boynton Beach, Florida.

Sarah E.C. Byrne made a generous donation to charity to have her name in this novel. She's a lawyer from Canberra, Australia, and a crime fiction aficionada.

Thank you Femmes Fatales for your encouragement and advice. Read our blog at femmesfatales.typepad.com. My fellow bloggers at the award-winning Kill Zone have given useful and entertaining writing advice. Read us at killzoneauthors.blogspot.com.

And finally, any mistakes are mine.

Any questions or comments? Please e-mail me at eviets@aol.com.

ABOUT THE AUTHOR

ELAINE VIETS has written 32 mysteries in four series: the bestselling Dead-End Job series, the cozy Josie Marcus Mystery Shopper mysteries, the dark Francesca Vierling mysteries, and the Angela Richman, Death Investigator series. With Angela Richman, Elaine returns to her hardboiled roots and uses her experience as a stroke survivor and her studies at the Medicolegal Death Investigators Training Course. Elaine was a director at large for the Mystery Writers of America. She's a frequent contributor to Alfred Hitchcock's Mystery Magazine and anthologies edited by Charlaine Harris and Lawrence Block. Elaine won the Anthony, Agatha and Lefty Awards.

FOR NEWS ABOUT
JABBERWOCKY
BOOKS AND AUTHORS

Sign up for our newsletter*: http://eepurl.com/b84tDz
visit our website: awfulagent.com/ebooks
or follow us on twitter: @awfulagent

THANKS FOR READING!

*We will never sell or giveaway your email address, nor use
it for nefarious purposes. Newsletter sent out quarterly.